ALice by ACCiDENT

Collins

An imprint of HarperCollinsPublishers

First published in the USA in 2000 by HarperCollins Children's Books,
a division of HarperCollins*Publishers*, 10 East 53rd Street, New York, NY 10022.

First published in Great Britain by Collins 2003
Collins is an imprint of HarperCollins*Publishers* Ltd,
77-85 Fulham Palace Road, Hammersmith,
London W6 8JB

The HarperCollins website address is:
www.harpercollins.co.uk

3 5 7 9 8 6 4 2

Text copyright © Lynne Reid Banks 2000
Illustrations by Tania Hurt Newton

The author and illustrator assert the moral right to be identified
as the author and illustrator of this work.

ISBN 0 00 714387 7

Printed and bound in England by
Clays Ltd, St Ives plc

For a very special person,
whom I love to distraxion.

SCHOOL NOTEBOOK

MY LIFE

by Alice Williamson-Stone

I am nine years and six months old and my name is Alice Elizabeth Williamson-Stone. I am medium tall with very long brown curly hair that I wear in a pigtail and dark brown eyes. I was born in Brighton and I lived there till a year ago. It's a lovely town with the Lanes and the pavilion which we visited twice with our school and the sea and the peer with a funfair on it and my favourite restaurant Pinocchio's and the marina where you can tickle flatfish and I wish we were back there, I don't like London as much (in some ways).

My mum is a professional single parent. I liked it better when she was on benefit cos she was always at home but Mum says she likes to work and at least she's got a good job and makes some money. Not that we feel any richer, we still never seem to have any to spare. Mum's always saying "You have to make hard choices if you're a single parent.

This is embarasing but I'm going to write it. When I was little I asked Mum where I came from (!!) and she said I came by accident. Then for quite a long time I used to say when I met people, "Hello I'm Alice, I came by accident." They used to give me very funny looks and Mum told me perhaps I shouldn't say that and I said why, isn't it true? Mum never tells lies to me. She didn't say anything. I didn't even know what came by accident ment then. I think I thought an accident was some kind of car or train or something that brought me!!!

Then I noticed that when people said accident it was usually something bad. Like a girl in my nursery class peed in her pants and the teacher said she'd had an accident. When I was staying with Gene (my grandma) once I knocked over a glass of orange juice that went on the table and dripped cold all over my legs and I was scared she'd be furious but she said, never mind it was an accident.

Then one day me and my mum saw a crowd in the street and she said don't look, there's been an accident. I asked what she ment and she said someone's been knocked down by a car. I started crying and she said what's wrong, and I wouldn't say for ages but then she made me, and I said, accidents are bad I don't want to be an accident, and she hugged me hard and said there are different kinds and you're the good kind. "You're a happy accident."

Later when I knew more, I figgered out that accidents are what happen when you're not expecting them and I said to Mum didn't you expect me? And she said, well I certainly knew you were coming. And I said, so how was I an accident? She said, "because I didn't plan you. I said didn't you want me? Then I got scared of what she'd say. And she said no I didn't, not at first. But when you were born and I held you I wanted you more than anything. You're the best thing that's ever happened to me. And I said, you mean the best accident and she hugged me and larfed and said yes.

After that I didn't mind being an accident but I stopped telling people I was because Mum said it was private and now I go really red when I think I told people that.

But lately I've found out it's not so good to be any kind of an accident whatever my mum says. It's mixed up with me being an accident that we lost

Gene. That's my grandma who liked me to call her by her first name because she said grandma made her feel old. At least that was part of it.

I can't hand this in. I'll have to tear the pages out and that means pages drop out of the back. I wish Brandy (Miss Brand, our teacher) had asked us to write a made-up story because I love making up stories almost as much as I love drawing.

It's just so stupid, asking us to write our lives for homework. It's not even a weekend!!! I remember enough things in my life to keep me writing for about a million hours. I don't write fast because my grandma muddled me up about writing, trying to teach me cursive. Just telling about <u>that</u> would take half an hour.

When I moaned about the homework, Brandy said she hadn't ment we should write our whole life story. She just ment the main things, like what we look like and where we were born and about our homes and families and pets and stuff. I said all my pets died and I don't know my family exept my mum. Miss Brand said what about that famous grandma of yours and I felt a pain inside as if I was going to cry and I said "I don't have her any more." Miss Brand said what Alice don't tell me she died too, and I didn't say anything but I wanted to say no she's not dead, only to us. But I couldn't write about that because it's private. Mum says I should never write about private things for school and she thinks nearly everything that happens out of school is private.

But I like the idea of writing about myself. This that I've written so far is for myself. When I've torn it out I'll selotape it into an old notebook from my old school. I'm going to watch The Simpsons now and then start my homework again in my proper book.

Later. The Simpsons was brilliant. I love Bart but my favourite is Lisa. I love her being so clever when Bart is so stupid (but he isn't really, for example he saved his aunt from being murdered) and I love the long words she uses. Lisa I mean. I could write for hours about The Simpsons. Describing every single episode. It's not just for kids. Mum keeps larfing and won't tell me what the joke is especially when Homer and Marge are in bed.

I don't want to do Miss Brand's homework, I want to go on writing private stuff. But Brandy will kill me so I have to. So I'll tear these pages out and start again. But first I'll write "special notebook private" on

my old one. That'll be for writing about my true
private life.

SCHOOL NOTEBOOK

MY LIFE

by Alice Williamson-Stone

I was born in Brighton and on April 8th I will be ten. I don't think I'm pretty but I have strait teeth and big eyes and my hair is nice but I wish Mum would let me have it cut (and have my ears perced) but she says I can't till I'm SIXTEEN!! My mum is a solicitor. I have no brothers or sisters. I have two grandmas and one grandad. I may have another grandad too. I have some aunts and an uncle and cousins but I don't see them exept once I met my Auntie Carla and my cousin James who's a baby and sweet but boring when they came to visit us from Liverpool. I used to have a pair of minicher hamsters and a goldfish called Jason because he was golden like the golden fleece. The hamsters were called Itchy and Scratchy after the cat and mouse in The Simpsons. They all died. I cried most about Jason, and I haven't had a pet since then. I had a Tamagochi cyberpet but that was yonks ago. I want another pet. I'd like a dog but I know it would be too hard to look after it and they cost too much to feed. But something small like another hamster or maybe a white rat. Rats are very soshable and like to stay in your pocket.

In Brighton we lived in a flat on a main road. I never went outside by myself because it was dangerous. Gene my grandma said I was a battery child, that's like chickens who are always kept indoors, but in London I'm a bit more free-range. We live in a house my grandma lent us. It's bigger than the flat and it's got a garden and it's in a quiet street so I can ride my bike and play outside, and there are other kids, but not the ones I go to school with. But I still think of our flat in Brighton as home. That's where my proper room is with most of my things in it including my bed and my hammock and my fairy doll and my big armchair where my stuffed animals live. All exept Benny my blue bear, I brought him with me of course. I wish we could go back there but we can't because Mum works in London and it's too far to commute. English is my second favourite subject after Art. I always get As in Art.

That's my life.

B+. It's good, Alice, and would have got an A if your punctuation had been better. I know, you get carried away, but presentation matters — <u>try harder</u>! And why are you doing this strange joined-up writing? Please PRINT. Spelling (not so bad this time) — copy 5 times each: pierced, miniature, sociable.

Special ~~SCHOOL~~ NOTEBOOK PRIVATE

My life? Well all I can think of that isn't private. Talk about boring, but it's what she asked for. I wrote it all in my grandma's kind of writing, joined up and with loops for the b's, h's, g's, j's, k's, q's, y's and l's. Little f's have two loops, top and bottom, they're a tail-letter <u>and</u> a tall-letter. I can't do the capital letters in Gene's kind of writing exept the F's and G's. I practised F's when she first showed me because they're fun to write, it's like drawing a fancy design, like this 𝓕 . Capital G's are fun too, you can do two kinds 𝓖 or 𝓰 . I like 𝓖 best of course but it's not very G-ish.

I've been sent up to bed. Mum got fed up with me because I keep talking about the row she had with Gene so she said "Go to bed and read, I want to watch TV." She watches TV alot. She used to read me bedtime stories but she stopped. She said because now I can read for myself but I think it's because I complained because she got sleepy in the middle and her voice sort of went away and I had to keep nudging her. She got really hurt feelings and wouldn't read to me any more even when she wasn't sleepy.

Gene used to read to me. She read really well because she's an actress, she did different voices for all the caracters in the stories. She used to sing songs to me too when I went to stay with her in the country. She knows millions of songs with all the words. I'm really upset with Gene but Mum says even if you get angry with people you should try to remember the good things about them. Mum said that for when I'm angry with <u>her</u>, but I'm using it for Gene. Only it doesn't work all the time cos the anger is too strong. Well it's not all being angry, it's mostly being sad because I miss her. Still who wouldn't be angry with a grandma who has a row with your mum and then doesn't see you any more.

When I wrote that last bit I started crying so I stopped. I cry alot when I think about Gene so I think I'll stop thinking about her.

* * *

I was quite pleased with getting a B+, and I copied the spellings, which I don't always. Only three, it's a miracle, I usually get a dozen, maybe the Brandy medsin is working. She is SO STRICT AND PICKY banging on about presentation. Putting in quote marks and paragraphs is just so <u>fiddly</u> I can't be bothered. After the lesson she kept me back and said "I want you to stop this silly show-off writing."

I said it's called cursive. She said I know what it's called but we don't do cursive writing in British schools any more it's too hard to learn. Gene told me she'd probably say that and what she means is it's too hard to <u>teach</u>. Gene said that for hundreds of years kids learnt to do cursive and do good penmanship and they still do it in America but here now they just do joined-up print which is babyish and a cop-out.

I said to Miss Brand "but I like writing cursive and Brandy said quite crossly "Well you can't, unless you can do it properly it looks like a spider that got drunk on ink. Everyone larfed and I felt a bit hurt. It didn't put me off though. I'm going to practise the capitals secretly. You can't join-up Brandy's kind of capitals. Gene said if you have to keep lifting your pen between letters you write much slower and that makes sense. I want to write fast because I'm going to write <u>alot</u>.

At least Brandy didn't make me copy my life story all out again. Nicola and Alexandra had to cos they got Cs. You have to if you get anything under a C+. But she said "<u>Basicly</u> it was good. You see you could write your life story." My life story will be ten years long in April. Till now it's only nine and a half years long. (It's true I don't remember the first three and only bits after that until I was about eight.)

I've decided I'm going to write my ortobiography in here in cursive in my special notebook. First I'll practise some cursive capitals. I've got them all written by Gene on a piece of paper with extra lines on it so the spider doesn't look so drunk. F and G first and then I'll do the others that aren't so fancy but they're still fancier than Miss Brand's boring print ones.

F G or *g*

A B C D E F G H I
J K L M N O P Q R
S T U V W X Y Z

The only one you can't join to the next letter is a P because it ends too high up.

I'm going to draw pictures in here too, I've just thought of it, it will be an ilustrated ortobiography. I'll start with a picture of Peony. She's my child minder's little girl so I see her every day after school. She's only eight but she's completely mad. She wears crazy clothes and hats with things stuck in them like the bottoms of old shoes and paper flowers and choclate rappers. She makes her mum buy her crazy clothes in jumble sales and she actully wears them outside like she cut two pairs of trowsers up and pinned the wrong legs together and she wears different shoes on each foot. Once she went to school in a mad outfit (she changed on the way behind a hedge in someone's front garden!!) and they sent her home only she couldn't go because they haven't got a phone so her mum couldn't come and get her so she wore all this funny gear all day, the other kids kept falling off their chairs larfing and the teacher was going bananas.

There. That's Peony in her odd legs and crazy hat and that silky blouse down to her knees. It's good.

I don't want to write about when I was very small because I did babyish things, maybe I will later. So I'll write about something interesting that I still think about and that's Pierre-Luc.

He was Mum's boyfriend and he was French. He was very nice and I liked him and Mum liked him. He came around alot and he used to take us for meals to Pinocchio's which was my favourite restaurant and it still is. We don't eat out much in London. Now Mum's working she's often too tired to go out <u>or</u> cook and besides she is still saving money so we eat mainly beans on toast and salads and sometimes we phone a number and they bring you pizzas to the door. But they're never as good as the ones we used to get in Pinocchio's. My favourites are margeritas. That's tomato and cheese. I'm not allowed to eat red meat because you can get mad cow disease. Every time I do something a bit silly Mum thinks I've got mad cow disease!! We're practically vegetarians exept for chicken (sometimes) and fish but I hate fish. (Exept tuna.)

Once when Pierre-Luc started coming around I asked Mum if he was my dad. She said NO and don't say that to him. That was the first time I remember asking her why my dad didn't live with us. She said "because he doesn't love me." I said why not, I love you, and she said you can't order love. He just didn't and he couldn't help it. I said so why is he my dad, and she said, "You'll understand better when you're older.

I was only about six then. I don't know if I understand better now. Gene said people shouldn't have babies if they aren't a couple. If they don't love each other and want to be together. When I told Mum that Gene said that, she didn't say anything but I could tell she was furious. When I asked her why she was upset she said, "That means she thinks I shouldn't of had you." Next time I saw Gene I asked her if that was true, and she wouldn't say so I nagged her to answer and she finally said I love you so I can't unwish you, but still it's not a good way to have a baby, you ought to be married first or at least have a partner."

I think about that alot. Especially since the Big Row. It's part of why I'm on Mum's side and against Gene. How can you like a person who thinks you shouldn't of been born (even if she is your grandma, I mean especially?)

Anyway back to Pierre-Luc. They used to kiss alot but they used to fratch alot too. Fratch is Mum's and my word for small quarrelling. I liked Pierre-Luc but I loved Mum much more so I was always on her side but I could see she was making him annoyed. I said don't pick on Pierre-Luc or he won't come around any more or do grown-up cuddling with you. Him being in the flat made me feel very safe.

Because once when he wasn't there we had a prowler. Mum went to draw the curtains on our french windows into the back garden and she saw him out there in the dark. He'd climed over the wall from the side street and he was just standing there looking in. Mum was so scared she screamed really loud and I got a bad fright and started to cry and ran and hid in my hammock. He jumped over the wall and ran away and Mum called the police but they never caught him and I didn't feel safe after that unless Pierre-Luc was staying the night. I always made Mum close the curtains even in the daytime in case the prowler came to watch us, and we just put on the lights. When Gene visited she always put on a funny deep voice and said "Ah! Stijian gloom!" Or "Darkness at noon." (I never found out what stijian means, Gene said she didn't know either but it sounds really gloomy.) Then she used to pull back the curtains which Mum thought was cheeky because it wasn't her flat, but I wasn't scared when Gene was there. After I was about eight I stopped being so scared but by then it was a habit with Mum and we only had the curtains open when Gene came so we had stijian gloom all day.

By that time Pierre-Luc had left for good. He never said goodbye. They had one last fratch and he said "You are always creeteesize me! Eef you feel like zat I weel leave and not come back." When he did leave and didn't come back I was angry with Mum and told her off. I said he was nice and he took us out and you made him go away. She said men have to respect me and I said he did respect you and she said no he didn't, not enough. I said why not and she said that's just how men are.

I suppose my dad didn't respect her enough as well as not love her. I have fights with my mum but I don't understand how anyone could not love and respect her.

I'll write a list of why she should be respected.

First she's a woman and women are better than men. They aren't so vilent and by far the most criminles are men. Women live longer and they have babies which you need to be strong for and it's nearly always the man who runs off when they've had them and the women stay.

Second she's done everything she's done by herself. She hasn't got a family to help her. My other grandma married a man who

No, I'm going to tell that part properly, like a story.

My mum grew up in Liverpool. She had a big sister called Dawn and a big brother called Robert and a younger sister Carla. She's the aunt I met, the one with baby James (he hasn't got a dad either). Mum's father was OK to the others but he used to pick on Mum and hit her all the time. I just can't imagine what my mum would do if some man tried to hit me, I think she'd kill him. She nearly killed a babysitter we had once who slapped me. But <u>her</u> mother just sat there. She let Big Pig get away with it and sometimes she even joined in. (Big Pig's what Mum calls him.)

Then one day when my mum was sixteen she was out shopping and she saw a man. He was walking down the street towards her. She looked at him and she couldn't believe it because he looked like her. He looked so like her she suddenly knew something. She knew the man who had picked on her and hit her all her life and that she thought was her dad wasn't her dad at all. <u>The man in the street was her dad</u>. Only by the time she knew this he'd gone past into the crowds.

She ran home as fast as lightning and burst in and there was her mum and she shouted at her, "Your Big Pig husband isn't my dad and why did you let me think he was?" and her mum was <u>shattered</u>. She said "How do you know?" and Mum said because I've just seen my real dad. And her mum burst out crying and locked herself in her bedroom.

Then the Big Pig came home and Mum had a good look. She saw him with <u>new eyes</u>. She'd sometimes wondered why she looked so different from him, when her brother and sisters were like him. (AND she was cleverer than all of them. She didn't tell me that but I know it's true because of what she did later.)

So anyway B.P. started shouting and swaring at her and putting her down and she said you can't talk to me like that any more because you're not my father." And he went mad and said I've always looked after you you ungreatful little something really rude, and she said all you've done was made me out to be a nothing and then he tried to hit her and <u>she</u> went mad and picked up a big kitchen knife and said if you touch me I'll use this and he swore at her more but he was really scared and her mum came running in acting crazy and tried to get the knife off her. They were all acting crazy.

In the end Mum's big sister Dawn who was really her half-sister came home and she got the knife away from Mum and calmed things down, but that night Mum packed some things and went out of their house where she'd always lived and she went to a friend's house from school and stayed there. After that she never went back home exept once to get her things. She got an after school and Saturdays job and paid her friend's parents for the room and later she got her A-levels and got into university which <u>no one else in her whole family ever had</u>. And that's one good reason why you have to respect my mum because most people of sixteen would of crawled home and just put up with it because they'd of been so scared of everything being different and being on their own.

My grandma Gene told my mum off when she found out she'd told me all this about her stepfather hitting her with his belt and about the knife and everything when I was only about five. I heard her when I was ment to be asleep. She said "How could you wish all that on to a little girl. But Mum said "Alice had to know about it to understand why we don't see my mother and why I would never ever go back to Liverpool." I'm glad now that she told me when I was young before I could imagine it properly. I kind of got used to it but when I think about it like now, I just want to go and do something really bad to Big Pig for hurting my mum and spoiling her child time and not respecting her. It makes me wish she'd stuck the knife right into him and made him scream like he did her when he hit her bare legs with his belt when she was only little just because she wasn't his little girl.

I'm writing this over days and days, not all at once. My cursive's getting better. I can write <u>much</u> faster now.

Today I drew a picture of my old room in Brighton in Art and got another A. It was fun drawing the hammock and I put Benny in it even though he's with me.

Now the number three reason why my mum deserves to be respected.

In my old school there were other girls in my class with single mothers and not one of them's mother was a professional exept one and she had her profession before she got divorced. They mostly either lived on benefit or had part-time jobs or low-paid jobs. My mum had me right after she finished university but just before I was born she passed her exams and got her degree but she was pregnant and living with the medical students so it was only a desmond.

That's a joke Mum told me. There's this famous black priest called Desmond <u>Tutu</u> in South Africa. And when you say you got a desmond at university it means you got a 2-2 degree. <u>2-2</u> like Tutu. A First is the best, then there's a 2-1, then there's a desmond which is third-best but for Mum it was brilliant because she was pregnant and didn't have anyone to help her.

She was living with five other students and they were all men medical students exept her. They drank loads of beer and they never ever washed up and the table that was for all of them was always covered with dirty dishes and jars of jam and beer tins and stuff so if you made room for a mug at one end, something fell off at the other end (Mum told me this like a big joke but I tried it once, I put every single dish and pot we had on our table in Brighton and then tried to push a mug on, and a glass fell off the other end!! Lucky it was a thick one so it didn't break.) and the place kept getting filthy and she was the only one who cared so she was the only one who cleaned up.

They often got drunk and noisy so she could hardly study or even sleep and they teased her rotten <u>and</u> they made sexist remarks. They even teased her if she stood up for herself. They wouldn't let her watch her favourite programmes on TV either, they only wanted to watch sport and other stupid stuff and if she argued they said this flat is a democracy and it's five votes to one. She says she still doesn't know the end of a really good old film called "The Letter" that starts with Betty Davis shooting someone because they just turned it off in the middle to watch stupid football.

When they found out she was pregnant though, they got a bit nicer and didn't let her lift things and didn't tease her and one of them used to bring her mugs of tea in bed in the mornings to stop her being sick. But they still got drunk and made a noise and a mess and it was really hard for her to study so that's why she got a desmond instead of a First which she could of I bet if things had been different, like she'd had a proper family to help her and a proper home.

But getting a degree doesn't mean you're a professional. You have to go on studying, and when I was about three Mum started studying to be a solicitor. It takes about four years only it took Mum five because she had to look after me. She was on benefit then because she didn't want to leave me and she couldn't afford proper child care. But she studied at home mostly after I was asleep.

Sometimes she had to go to classes and take exams and then she had to leave me with a neighbour. Mrs Blewitt. I still remember her <u>really</u> well. She was old and fat and her flat smelled. Mum said it was her dog but I think it was her. She was always <u>creepy-crawly</u> in front of Mum and said things like "Alice and I are going to wonderland today aren't we dearie? but when Mum went away she changed and got really cross and crabby. She used to stick me on her mouldy old sofa covered with dog-hairs and say "don't you move miss or Lady will bite you. Lady was the dog. She never bit me but I always thought she would and I was dead scared of dogs for years until Gene and Copper cured me. Copper was Gene's dog, a water spaniel, much bigger than Lady and when I first went to Gene's and Grandad's cottage I was scared to death of her but I'm not scared of her any more even when she jumps up on me. I wonder how she is I haven't seen her for ages and when I saw her last which was last summer she was going to have puppies. Last summer was really good but I don't want to write about it because it gives me that pain. I wish I wish I wish Gene and Mum hadn't quarrelled. A real quarrel not a fratch.

Mrs Blewitt brought me my lunch that was always

jam sandwiches on a plate to the sofa but she didn't talk to me exept to tell me don't move. She would shuffle around and dust all her dinky little ornaments and go into her bedroom for a lay-down. She didn't have a TV. She played the radio all day, but it was all talk radio and I didn't understand it much. I was so bored I slept most of the time.

She always told Mum in her creepy-crawly voice that we'd been for a nice walk but we never went out exept once she had to take Lady to the vet. She didn't hold my hand crossing the road like Mum always did because she was holding Lady and saying goo-goo things to her like poor little girlikins got a pain in her wickle toofipeg. (Yuck.) She had to leave Lady there. When we got back she made me go to the sofa, but when she was having her lay-down I got off the sofa and walked about the room and took some of her little china animals and played with them on the floor. I felt quite safe because Lady couldn't bite me from the vet's, but she came out and caught me. Mrs Blewitt did, not Lady. Mrs B was so mad she trod on a china elefant on the floor and then she said "Look what you made me do, I ought to beat you black and blue!!!"

She picked me up and threw me back on the sofa,

really threw me, like a doll or something. It didn't hurt much but it scared me so badly I threw up, and then she shouted and screamed at me and made me clean it up. After that the sofa stank of my sick.

I was going to tell Mum that time, but in the end I didn't. I never told how Mrs Blewitt changed or about the sofa and Lady. I even made things up that we'd done. Of course I know now it was stupid but I was only five and I thought Mrs Blewitt would know I'd told and would tell Lady to bite me next time I was there. So I stayed on the sofa all day exept when I had to pee and then I called Mrs Blewitt to take me to the loo and make Lady stay in her basket.

Around that time I got different. I just sulked and got angry with Mum alot and had tantrums. I threw things and shouted at her and wouldn't go to bed. That's when I started really fussing about what I ate. I started peeing my bed and even peed on the floor in our flat. I didn't know why I was doing it. Mum got very worried about me. She asked if there was ever a man at Mrs Blewitt's but there wasn't.

Then she took me to Brenda. Brenda was my therapist. I used to go there once a week to play and I loved it there. There was a sandpit and dolls and things to draw with. I had toys at home but it was nice to have different ones at Brenda's and Brenda sort of played with me. She would ask me to pretend that one of the dolls was me and one was Mummy and there was a man doll that Brenda said was daddy. He made me giggle because he had a willy under his trowsers. I said I don't have a daddy but she said, everyone does, pretend this doll is your daddy. Would you like to talk to him? I said no. She said try, and I said hello daddy, and the doll just lay there with his willy and I couldn't think of anything for him to say back.

But I knew how to make up plays with dolls because I used to do it all the time with Gene. So I made the man doll be Pierre-Luc (he was still around then). I made them fratch and then I was going to make them kiss and make up like they really did but I stopped because even when I was only five I knew that grown-up cuddling is private.

One time I pretended that the woman doll was Mrs Blewitt and I told her I thought she was the meanest person in the world and that she smelled and then I buried her in the sand. She said don't don't and I did her voice, like Gene did when we played to make it seem real, and dropped wooden bricks on her. I asked if there was a dog doll (to be

Lady) and Brenda gave me a stuffed dog. I made Lady try to dig Mrs Blewitt up while I threw more sand on her with my other hand. In the end I made Lady growl and bite me and I dropped a big wooden brick on her and killed her.

But that went wrong because Brenda thought I'd killed Mummy!!! And I said of course not, that's not Mummy. Then she said poor old dog, and I didn't say anything. Then she said what dog is that? I said it's just a dog. She said have you got a dog and I said NO THANKS I hate dogs. She said well you certainly seem to hate that one.

I think maybe she asked Mummy about the dog and Mummy caught on because I never had to go to Mrs Blewitts after that. When Mum had to go to classes she used to take me to the council playgroup. It was rough and noisy there but it was better than Mrs Blewitt and I stopped wetting my bed and only had a tantrum sometimes. I kept on fussing about food though.

Another time Brenda said I should draw pictures of my family and I drew me in bed with Mummy. It was a really good drawing, I did the whole living room with the futon unfolded and I put some of my pictures on the walls. Brenda said do you and

Mummy sleep in the same bed and I said the same futon. She said don't you have a bed of your own and I said yes but it's wobbly and besides it's upstairs and I like to sleep downstairs where Mummy is. I didn't tell Brenda how I lay awake sometimes feeling scared of prowlers and wishing she'd stop studying and cuddle in with me. Sometimes I made myself cry so she'd come to bed early.

I was eight before Gene bought me a new bed. She said it was obseen to be sleeping with my mum at my age. Mum wanted Gene to give me the bed so she didn't say anything but later she told me obseen means something dirty and that Gene had no right to say that even though she didn't exactly mean it, Mum said actresses use exajerated language. She said "Gene always hints I'm not bringing you up properly and it's none of her dam business. She should just stick to being a grandma."

I haven't written anything for three weeks. I wanted to write only about my life till now but my life keeps getting new things to write about. I wish it would stay still for a bit and let me catch up. The big news is, Gene wrote to us to say we have to leave this house because she's given it to my father.

My father's got married. It was in the letter and Mum cried and I snatched the letter and read it. Lucky I can read cursive. I asked Mum if she was crying because she loved my dad and was angry he married another person and she said "I don't know. I suppose I always dreamed he might come back one day and make us a family but I knew deep down that he wouldn't."

I said but what does it mean if Gene's given him the house, does it mean he'll come and live here?" Mum said "No. Your dad married a Dutch woman and he's gone to live in Holland." I wondered how she knew but I suppose Gene told her. She and Gene used to be friends even though they fratched sometimes. Once Gene called Mum her daughter-out-law. Mum told me that means a woman who is NOT married to your son.

I said, "So why has Gene given my dad our house if he doesn't want to live in it?" and Mum said houses are useful for earning money from rent. I said don't we pay rent for this house, because we did at Brighton, Mum was always on about finding the rent, and Mum said no, Gene said we could stay in it for nothing. So I said well we could pay Dad rent, and Mum shouted through her crying, us pay him, I'd rather die than give him money. He should give us money. I said why and she said mentenance. I said what's mentenance and she said, "it's the money fathers are supposed to pay for their children even if they don't live with them. That's the law. Now please stop asking questions because this is bad news and I have to think it through."

I said will we go back to Brighton and she said, we can't, you've started school here and my work's in London and we can't commute, it's impossible. Then she just <u>shouted</u> "God I hate that bloody woman she makes me just want to die or kill someone!" She used to like Gene, sort of, but she hates her now. I get very scared when my mum gets like that. I remember about the knife and Big Pig and think she might really get vilent.

Brandy always said you should give background in a story. So I am going to be calm (not like Mum) and give the background.

Mum told me that when I was about three and things were really hard before she was a professional, she decided I needed a grandma and she wrote to Gene and asked her if she would be my grandmother. Gene'd never even seen me then and she hadn't seen my mum since before I was born.

Mum was really nervous after she sent the letter. She thought Gene might write back and say get lost or something worse but she didn't. She rang Mum (in Brighton this was) and they had a row strait off because Mum had called me Williamson-Stone on my birth certificate. Stone is her name and Williamson is my father's name and Gene's too. Gene said I had no right to that name because Mum wasn't married to my dad and she said Mum'd stolen it. Of course that's stupid, you can't steal a name and you can call your child anything you like, she could've called me Alice Pokémon or Alice Peanut Butter Sandwich if she'd liked but Gene didn't see it like that so she said at first that she didn't agree to be my grandmother.

But then one day she just turned up outside our door. I found out later that Gene had always been thinking about me since I was born and even before, when she'd come to see Mum at the digs with the medical students and told her off for being pregnant. She said it would spoil my dad's life and she called my mum a little tart.

I think it's weird that such a sweet name is really bad, it means a woman who has lots of boyfriends and that was <u>really</u> unfair because my mum'd only ever had one boyfriend then and that was my dad who was at university with her. She was afraid of men because of the Big Pig. My dad was very gentle and she trusted him. Now she says you can never trust men, even Pierre-Luc who was gentle too and really liked her but she got rid of him because of the respect. Since then she hasn't had a boyfriend at all so it was really bad of Gene to call her a little tart, she's NOT.

Anyway so she turned up in Brighton and Mum was in a state because the flat was a mess and I was in scruffy clothes and we hadn't much to eat in the flat because Mum hadn't been shopping and Gene asked for coffee and there wasn't any. Mum sort of lost her head and thought giving Gene coffee was the <u>main thing</u> and she dashed out to the shop and left Gene with me.

I wasn't used to strangers and I started crying (I don't remember this but Gene told me afterwards) and Gene got nervous and said "I can't stand this I'm afraid, I'm off and she went upstairs which is where the front door is and I heard a door shut and I thought she'd gone. I was never left alone when I was little and I was so scared that I just froze up. The minute I stopped crying Gene came back down. She walked back in and said that's better, now that we can hear ourselves think let's read a story. I stood looking at her and she said, Do you know who I am? I'm your grandmother, your father's mother. My name's Eugenie but you can call me Gene." I said "I hate you."

I was saying that alot just then, I didn't really know what it ment but I knew it upset grown-ups. But she wasn't upset she was quite cheerful. She said "Oh do you, well in that case I hate you right back." Nobody had ever said that to me. Mostly grown-ups said something like oh dear, or no you don't really. It gave me a shock when she said she hated me back. Then she said you've got some terrific books here. Which do you like best?" I picked up a book Mum had been reading to me (she read to me alot then). Grandma said, "Wow, Greek myths, those are my favourite too, which one shall we read?" And I said Jason and the golden fleece and she read it and then I said I've got a goldfish called Jason and she said "Show me" so we looked at Jason and she said "He needs his tank cleaning" and then she began talking to him and saying funny things for him to say back, like "Is anyone out there, I can't see you through all this green stuff, and she made him cough and sneeze, and when Mum came back with the coffee we were larfing.

The first thing I said to Mum was "Jason says he needs his tank cleaning" and Mum looked embarased and went to make the coffee. I went into the kitchen and told Mum that Gene said she hated me. Mum staired at me as if she didn't believe she'd heard right and Gene said from the other room well you don't expect me to love someone who doesn't love me but it's too early to decide what we feel. I peeped at her and she winked at me and I thought she doesn't really hate me. (I sort of remember that now, it's funny how you remember things when you're writing them, like photos.)

After she'd had coffee she said "I feel better now, let's go out for dinner, where shall we go, and I shouted Pinocchio's! And Mum said "sh Alice." But we went. We walked there and on the way Gene took my hand. I said "I hate you" again because I just didn't believe she'd say I hate you back in front of Mum, but she did, and snatched her hand away. Then I said "I love you." I didn't then but I was testing. And she said "I love you back" and took my hand again. We kept saying I hate you I love you all the way to Pinocchio's and taking hands and untaking them and the last thing we said as we turned into Pinocchio's was I love you. I never said I hate you to her again. Even since the row I don't hate her, even now she wants to throw us out of our house. Well, it's her house but we're living in it. I don't understand her and I feel angry and sad often but I don't hate her. I think Mum does though.

Mum says if something hurts you inside you ought to look into it so I will. After the wonderful summer I had staying with Gene and Grandad and going to Spain and everything and Gene talking to me all the time like a grown-up and telling me how much she loved me I felt really close to her and I thought Grandad was beginning to love me a bit too, he didn't tell me off so much as he usually did and gave me a really good hug when I left.

Gene drove me back to London and we were singing to the tape and we got stopped for speeding. The policeman was really snotty to her and after he'd gone she felt so bad she sat in the car and cried and I had to comfort her and tell her it was all right. She asked me not to tell Mum but Mum always says no secrets and I knew I would so in the end Gene told her. I'd never seen Gene ashamed before and it made me love her more because everyone makes mistakes and I stood there with my arms around her while she confessed to Mum and said she was sorry.

Mum said "You could have killed Alice, and Gene said, yes, it was terrible of me, we were rollicking along and I didn't notice, and Mum said if I never let her go in the car with you again would you blame me, and Gene said no, you'd be well within your rights. And then I said "it was only once and if I can't go in the car how can I go to stay in the country" and Mum and Gene looked at each other and I felt something. Something bad between them that I'd felt once or twice but only when Mum and I were talking about Gene, not when she was there. It was, like, Mum really needed Gene but she didn't like her and she was glad to have something to put her down with. But in the end Mum just said well promise not to speed ever again.

She'd got this good job while I'd been in the country. It was with a private solicitors that had clients that were mainly criminles. I was frightened when she told me because I thought she'd be with horrible vilent people like lawyers on TV but she said she wouldn't, she'd be working in the office and only have to go to court sometimes, she said criminles aren't dangerous when they're in court. She was so pleased to have found a good job, she took me out for an Indian meal to celebrate and I had chicken tikka masala.

But it took two hours to get to her office from Brighton and two hours back and I had to stay in school from 7.30 in the morning to 7.30 in the evening which was horribly boring and Mum was getting exorstid.

So that was when Gene said we could live in this house. It was hers and Grandad's then. She said we could use it because she'd made alot of money from acting a big part in a film and bought another place in London, a flat. She said we could stay in this house for a bit and she cleaned it all up for us, she really worked hard and she made the garden nice too. She even bought Mum a big desk and a long mirror so Mum could make sure she looked nice for going to work.

Mum complained quite alot about the house which I didn't understand. She said the bathroom wasn't as nice as ours which it wasn't. We had a very big one in Brighton. And there were some places where it needed decorating but no worse than ours. And she was cross when Gene asked her to keep the lawn mode. She said "I'm not a jobbing gardener." I thought that was bad and I told her off later. I said why aren't you more greatful to Gene for letting us live here?" and she said, Gene isn't doing it just to be kind. She's doing it because she wants me to keep this job. I said why, and she said, because she doesn't want me to give your dad's name to the DSS.

The DSS is the place that gives you money if you're poor or haven't got a job. But I didn't understand the rest. I said what if you did, and she said, "They'd get after him to give us some money. I said, "Why should he," and she said, "Because he's your father and fathers are supposed to pay for their children." I said so why doesn't he, and she said, "Because he doesn't want to. He doesn't think it's his responsibility. I said why not. At first she didn't want to answer, but I said "Tell the truth the whole truth and nothing but the truth." So then she said "Because he didn't agree that I should have you." I said, "You mean he didn't want me," and she said "No he didn't." I felt funny about that, not sad or angry, just funny. I asked her what she thought, if he should pay mentenance, and she said what counted was that we needed money and that the law was on our side.

* * *

Something really bad happened today. It's just the sort of secret Mum said I should never keep from her but I'll have to. I'll write it in here and then I'll hide this. I'd die if she saw it it would ruin everything, I might have to leave my school.

I haven't told about Sharon. She's my child minder Mum pays to pick me up every day after school. School ends at 3.30 and Mum can't come for me until at least 6 sometimes later. Mum says if she doesn't agree to work late sometimes she will be fired because all the men lawyers do and that's why it's hard for single mothers in a law practiss.

Sharon looks after some preschool kids while their parents work. At home time she brings them all to my school for a walk and then we go back to her flat and she gives me my tea and I'm supposed to play until Mum comes. This would be very boring exept for Peony. She's the one who wears the crazy clothes, Sharon's daughter. She goes to a local school, not private, and she's allowed to <u>walk to school by herself</u> which Mum thinks is terrible because she's only 8 and it's a rough part of London. Peony is fun and good at thinking up games specially dress-up ones but she's crazy and maybe even bad. I found that out today for certain.

Mum says I am not to <u>move</u> from the school yard <u>ever</u> until I'm picked up. Sharon knows I'm not allowed out in the streets alone. Well, today I waited and waited and Mrs Devereau (our headmistress) came out and asked me if I wanted her to phone my Mum at work but I said no. I mustn't ring Mum at work exept in a <u>dier emerjency</u>. So she left, and I waited more till everyone else had gone home. I felt very lonely and then I saw Peony coming dordling up the street.

I was releeved but mad too. I said "Where's your mum?" and she said "One of the little kids fell down so she sent me to fetch you." I didn't know what to say so I said I've been waiting and waiting, where have you been and she said "I went on the rob" and I said what's that and she said "look." She took a box out of her pocket. It had sent in it in a pretty bottle. I staired at it and looked at Peony and she had a sort of cocky smile and suddenly I knew what on the rob ment.

I said "you never stole it, Peony!" and she said "course I did, it was easy. It's for my mum's birthday and I nicked a card too, look." I was so shocked. I remembered Gene saying she hated thieves. She said stealing's such a mean nasty crime. Peony said "Mum said I was to take you to the shops and buy stuff for tea so come on" and I said I can't till your mum comes and she said, "Then you'll wait for ever" and she walked off!!!

What could I do, I had to go with her but my heart was pounding all the time because if Mum knew me and Peony were alone in the street she would go right up the wall. It got worse because when we went to buy the stuff for tea she stole two Penguins and a Yorkie bar and pushed them up her sweater AND she kept 50p for herself out of her mum's change. AND THEN she wouldn't take me back to Sharon's strait away. We went window shopping and she kept teasing me showing things she'd like to rob and we didn't get back till nearly 5.

I was so scared all the time that something really bad would happen like some man would kidnap us or that a policeman would arrest us for stealing. I thought Sharon would kill us for staying out, but she wasn't even angry with Peony when we got back but she said, "Better not tell Mum you were out alone."

That's just the kind of secret I knew not to keep but this time I had to, and when Mum came Sharon was winking at me and I had to pretend nothing special had happened. I've never lied to her properly before. But if I'd told I bet she would stop Sharon being my minder and I don't know what would happen then. It took Mum ages to find anyone to child-mind me. I might have to leave my school and go to a local one like Peony with boys and fights and bullies. And maybe drugs. I went to a local school in Brighton until Gene sent me to a private one. I hated it, I was bullied alot and there were too many of us in the class and it was always noisy and I didn't learn much.

I hated not telling Mum what happened with Peony and keeping that secret has made me withdraw a bit – that's what Mum calls it when she sort of gets all quiet, like she's somewhere else. And I'm worried because I don't know what's going to happen. Mum won't talk to me about it but I know we're going to have to move from Gene's house, I mean my dad's, and I might have to leave my school anyway and all my friends because maybe we'll have to go back to Brighton and Mum won't be able to commute so she'll lose her job and go back on benefit and then she'll sit at home alot and think about how my dad isn't paying mentenance.

SCHOOL NOTEBOOK

THE SECRET

by Alice Williamson-Stone

A girl's mother told her not to have secrets. She said secrets were bad because if something wasn't bad, why have a secret about it? By the way the girl's name was Carmen.

Carmen said, "What if it's a nice secret like a surprise party?" Her mum said "That's different, that's the exeption. But if someone tells you to keep a secret from me, you mustn't."

One day at school Carmen's best friend Laura wanted to tell her a big secret about one of the other girls. Carmen said "I will have to tell my mum" so Laura larfed at her and wouldn't tell her the secret. She told everybody else though exept the girl of course. By the way the girl's name was Sophie. Nobody liked Sophie much because she was different from them she came from some other country and didn't speak much English.

At break everyone was wispering and looking at Sophie. Sophie and Carmen were the only ones not in on the secret. Sophie started to cry and Carmen felt sorry for her she went up to her and said "Let's play scissors paper and stone." Sophie looked <u>like</u> she'd never heard of it but Carmen showed her and they played all through break and Carmen began to like Sophie a bit even though she was strange.

After break Laura said "you wouldn't play with her and be her friend if you knew the secret." Carmen said "I don't care about your old secret." Laura said "OK I'll tell it to you then. Carmen walked away but Laura followed her and made her listen.

"She's not supposed to be in Britain she's a refugee and her parents are locked up for sneaking in in a big truck. She lives with a council foster mother." Carmen said "How do you know?" Laura said, "it was in the papers and my mum showed me. There was a picture of her and her parents and what's worse is they're gipsys."

Carmen said "So what" and Laura said "My mum said they are fludding in and we have to pay for them because they don't want to work." Carmen said that's not Sophie's fault and Laura got annoyed and said "Anyway gipsys are dirty and lazy and we don't want her in our school. And they steal so look out if you're going to be her friend."

Carmen didn't know what to say so she just walked away.

Is this based on a true story, Alice? It certainly reads like it. But I don't like the end. Did Carmen just abandon Sophie? Your paragraphing is still not right: new paragraph when people speak. Spellings: exception, except, flooding, gypsy, gypsies. And, Alice, I beg you not to write "like" instead of "as if". I've underlined the place.

B+. Spelling much improved!

Special ~~SCHOOL~~ **NOTEBOOK** PRIVATE

It <u>was</u> a true story it happened in my old school in Brighton. The names were true except Carmen who was me. The story ended the way it did. I didn't <u>exactly</u> abandon Sophie, she left because her parents were sent back where they came from. When I told Mum about it she said Laura's secret was the sort of nasty secret that hurts people. She said "I wish you'd stayed friends with her poor little thing it's terrible they were sent back to Romania." I asked Mum if gypsies are dirty and lazy and she said just about like everyone else, some are some aren't, but gypsies are usually poor and dispised and that makes it hard for them to live like other people.

Today I had a letter from Gene. It started as just a nice friendly letter about the play she's touring in (she sent a postcard from Leeds) but then she tried to explain why she's throwing us out of the house. I'll stick that bit in here.

I don't know what your mother has told you about why I want you to leave the house. I'd like to explain our side. I invited Mummy to stay in it _for a short time_ while she found somewhere in London to live, so she wouldn't have to commute from Brighton. I did everything I could to make sure you'd be happy and comfortable there. But _I never dreamt that you would still be living there nine months later_. Grandad is very cross with me because we've given the house to our son and his wife as a wedding present. But we've given them a white elephant — that means, something expensive and useless.

So now it is up to me to get Mummy to move out so it can be rented properly and be useful to our son, and not a burden. I expect Mummy thinks he owes her and should let her go on living there free, but that's not fair. Daddy doesn't owe her anything, and if he did, everything we've given you in the past five years would have paid the debt. Not that I begrudge you any of it. You know I love you to distraction. Nothing has changed that. I miss you every single day.

I must think about this, but I can't because there's bad news too. I can't believe it but Gene has sent Mum a lawyer's letter to make her get out of this house.

I said to Mum "You really really made her mad at us." Mum said "Stop it Alice, it's not all my fault. She made me lose control. And as for the house, mainly she wants it for <u>him</u>." I asked if we had to leave right away and Mum said "we'll leave when I'm good and ready." I said can she make us leave and Mum said "she can try to evict us but that takes time. I could take your father to court and say we should stay in this house because it's his and he owes us mentenance." I said "But he's in Holland" and she said "Yes, that's a problem. But if he ever comes back to England I'll take him to court."

Later I thought about why she didn't take him to court before he went to live in Holland if the law is on her side. I asked her and she said she hadn't wanted to get him then, because Gene was helping us, but <u>now</u> she wants to get him. But she can't because the law isn't on our side in Holland and we have to find another place to live.

* * *

Last night I heard Mum talking on the phone. I couldn't hear the words but I could tell she was not just talking to a friend. So I crept out on to the landing to listen. It took me about five minutes to relise she was talking to <u>my dad</u>. I couldn't believe it. She must of phoned him to Holland. She was saying he should let us have this house because he owed us and that he was my father and he was responsible for helping us. I wished I could hear what he said back but anyway Mum did most of the talking. She really went on at him, really critisising like with Pierre-Luc only much worse. I wanted to stop her because I just <u>knew</u> it wasn't going to work. Nobody does what you want them to if you go on at them, that's what she's always telling me. After about half an hour I got so sleepy I had to go back to bed. She was still going on at him. I wondered why he didn't just put the phone down like Gene sometimes did with Mum when she went on too long.

When I was back in bed just before I fell asleep I thought, if my dad tells Gene what Mum said to him, how she slagged him off about not looking after us and nagged him to give us the house, Gene will be more against her than ever, because my dad is her son like I'm Mum's daughter and mothers are always on their kids' side.

Gene used to be my number two person after Mum but she's not any more. You can't have a Number One and a Number Two who don't like each other. You've just got to choose and of course for me it's Mum. I haven't really got a Number Two now.

I'm going to make a list of all the things Gene did for me when she was my Number Two.

She bought me two bikes – one for the country and one for here – and clothes and took me to the ballet at Covent Garden (Copelia) and we had smoked samon sandwiches and to lots of plays at the Unicorn and the Polka, and to a real opera ("Carmen" – my favourite) and we did lots of other things together like go in boats on lakes, and once we went to the fair on the peer at Brighton with Mum, and Gene did the rides with me because Mum didn't want to. Even Mum said Gene was very sporty and brave for her age (she's actully very old, she's 66).

The best things though were she taught me to swim and ride a bike, which was hard work because she had to run after me holding the saddle, and she taught me to read. She told me about the magic E and gave me lots of books. One was called "Purple Hair I

Don't Care" and that was the first book I read by myself, well sort of. I knew most of it by heart I admit.

Gene came to London to take me out when Mum needed a rest and between oh pairs. Mum didn't like oh pairs, she had rows with them and they didn't usually stay long. Then there was last summer. I spent most of it with Gene and Grandad in the country.

I haven't written much about Grandad because I didn't feel comfortable with him like I did with Gene (most of the time). I always thought he didn't really like me and only put up with me because Gene made him. Not that he ever said anything, he was quite nice to me, but it was more like polite than loving.

I know Gene and him used to fratch about me sometimes. Once I was coming down the stairs at their cottage and I heard Grandad say, "You spoil that child rotten." I stopped and listened, I couldn't help it, I wanted to hear what Gene said back. What she said was, "I <u>don't</u> spoil her, I just try to make things up to her because she hasn't got a father." Grandad said, "That was her dam mother's choice. (My heart jumped when he said that.) What choice did <u>he</u> have? Nobody told her to have a baby." Gene said, "Nobody told our son to be so selfish and careless." I didn't know what she ment but it made me feel really bad, like I had two bad parents. I crept upstairs again to my room. Luckily Copper was there and I cried on her and she licked me better. Later of course I pretended I hadn't heard and everything was normal. That was one time I didn't tell Mum everything afterwards like I usually always did.

They've got a swimming pool that I learnt to swim in when I was six and a big garden with a den that Gene made me in some bushes and a vegtable garden where I was allowed to pull up carrots and dig up potatoes and pick peas. They have a horsey neighbour called Marion. She lives in a manor house and has ponies and I learnt to ride there on an old pony called Biddy. She's 26 years old now but she can still trot-on and I've had lots of rides on her ever since I was five.

Last summer I learnt to rise to the trot and I cantered a bit but that was because Biddy took off. She's not a bit like an old lady pony, Marion says she has a will of iyon. When I told Mum this she said, "just like another old lady we know." She ment Gene.

Marion's daughter Jessie is three years older than me and she wouldn't play with me last summer cos she's a teenager nearly, but she did when I first started to go there. She has a swing and a slide and a tree house which was brilliant. At first I was even scared to clim the ladder but Jessie made me. Marion and Gene would bring picnics up to us and we had dolls and animals tea parties with little tea cups and stuff. Up among the leaves, it was brilliant. I used to dream I was up there in a kind of fairyland or heaven or some place far away from everything having adventures. (Gene used to say I didn't have enough adventures because Mum was too frightened about me being safe.)

In the Christmas holidays I went although I always came back in time to have Christmas with Mum cos she would be lonely. Once Gene asked her to come. There was no room in the cottage so Mum stayed with Marion at the manor, and came to be with us every day, but it didn't work. She went into one of her funny moods and suddenly after about three days she was gone when I woke up. Gene said she'd walked from the manor in the night and asked to be taken to the railway station. I could see Gene was annoyed. She said you've got a moody old mum I must say. I phoned Mum strait away (she was home by then) and I told her off but she said "I'm sorry Alice, I couldn't stand it. I felt really antsy there." That means ants in your pants but she ment, not comfortable. The manor is very very comfortable and she had a double bed and her own bathroom and everything, but I think she ment comfortable inside, about being around Gene and Grandad. (Specially Grandad who I could tell didn't like her.)

She told me to stay on so I did and we did the Christmas play at the manor like we did for three years. I played a spoilt princess one year and I was a snow-girl the next year and a space invader last year. Jessie's friends used to be in them too. Gene wrote the plays and was the producer, she was very strict at rehearsals but if she hadn't of been the plays wouldn't of been any good. Jessie's dad always played Rudolph the red-nosed reindeer and another girl's dad did Santa and he was always a bit drunk and never knew his lines, and Gene got furious. I heard her in the kitchen really shouting at Santa for being drunk but she never got mad at me. She treated me the same as the other kids at rehearsals but later she told me I was a real actress like her and a good singer (there were always songs Gene made up, I loved those, but my best thing was helping paint the scenery on big sheets of paper. I helped Marion do a really good snow scene the year we did "The Snow Children".)

The last time I was there at Christmas I found out something. It was when I told Gene one night when she was kissing me goodnight that I'd rather stay with her over Christmas than go back to Mum. Mum gets nervous at Christmas. She doesn't like spending money on a tree and decorations and stuff because she never had a proper Christmas when she was little and I knew I'd have more fun and maybe more presents if I stayed. Gene does Christmas really well.

Gene said, "darling I'd love like mad to keep you here but you can't stay. Mummy would be very lonely, and besides." I said besides what, and Gene said well, Christmas is a time when children come home to their parents, even grown-up children. I didn't know what she ment at first and she wouldn't say any more but just as I was going to sleep it kind of burst inside my head. She ment that my dad was coming home.

I jumped up and ran downstairs where Gene and Grandad were watching television and shouted "Is my dad coming?" and Grandad got up and said, "Off to bed!" and pretended to chase me, but I saw from Gene's face I was right.

I thought so much about my dad coming I couldn't sleep and when I was ment to be going home, which was the day before Christmas Eve, I pretended to be ill so I wouldn't have to go. It wasn't for presents now it was so I could stay and meet my dad. But Gene just touched my forehead and looked at my tung and then said, "good try Alice but it's no go I'm afraid." She was on to me, she knew me so well.

Mum came on the train to collect me. While me and Gene waited on the platform for her train to come, I was upset because I knew my dad was coming, but Gene said, "Alice, I know it's hard but all the stastistiks say it's much worse to see your dad only every now and then than not at all." And then she said "It's better if you just don't think about him."

I said "but I think about him alot and she said "If you had a picture of him in your head or if you'd ever been with him you'd think about him much more. I turned very red because of something that had happened the summer before, and so she wouldn't notice I said "Just tell me something about him." Gene didn't talk for a bit but then she said he's a very sweet person. He made a big mistake once in his life but he didn't deserve to have to pay for it for ever." I said but he might love me if he met me and she said that's just what I'm afraid of, and that was all she would say. Then Mum's train came.

On the train going back to Brighton I told Mum the whole conversation in a very complaining way and Mum didn't say anything for a long time and then she said, "Gene's right this time, with dads it's all or nothing."

Well, it wasn't quite nothing with me.

The reason I blushed so hard before was that I do have a photo. Last summer I'd noticed that at the manor there were lots of pictures of Jessie mostly riding ponies and I thought of all my school photos my mum puts up among the ones I paint. I thought, other mothers keep pictures of their children about their house and there are no pictures of my dad at the cottage, why not?

And then I noticed some places on the walls where pictures might of been taken down. And one day when Grandad was at work and Gene was gardening I poked about in cupboards and draws and I found a picture of my dad in a frame. I just knew it was him. It wasn't like when my mum saw her dad in the street in Liverpool. He didn't look like me. But I just looked into his eyes in the photo and I knew he was my dad. He looked so gentle and nice just the way Mum said. And he was handsome.

I just sat for a long time looking at it and I thought you're my father. You're my father. And he looked back at me and said yes I am and I'm sorry. I remembered when Brenda had said I should talk to the man doll and I couldn't but I could talk to the photo and it answered. I said "where are you and why can't I see you?" and he said "when you're older perhaps we'll meet and I'll try to explain." I said "do you love me?" but he didn't answer that.

I put the photo back in the draw and I went on poking about and I found an album and there were lots of pictures in there. They were under that clear stuff that you peal off so it was easy to take one. It wasn't as good as the one in the frame but if I'd taken that I knew Gene would notice, so I sneaked an album one and hid it in my suitcase in a secret pocket. I felt very bad about stealing it because Gene often said, "I hate a thief." I just hoped she wouldn't find out and for a long long time it sat in my stomach like pizza when it's not cooked but I thought it wasn't fair that I didn't even know what he looked like.

And sometimes I take the picture out and stair at it and talk to it and sometimes he answers. But the hard questions like do you love me he doesn't answer. I know why, because how can he love me when he doesn't know me. I wonder alot if he's got a picture of me. I don't see how he could have, unless he's stolen one from Gene the way I did.

I've been thinking about Gene. I'm trying to remember good things, to stop from thinking maybe she's forgetting me. I'll write about last summer.

I spent most of it in the country with Gene and Grandad. It was good, I did a craft and acting course in Bayport and swam and rode and Marion taught me to trot on Biddy and Gene and me listened to music tapes (my favourite was "Carmen Jones" and I learnt all the words and Gene and I sang them together). And Gene gave me writing lessons and we read to each other and she gave me comprehension tests. Then she got a job acting.

Gene is a famous actress and plays big stage parts but this was a small part in a Spanish movie, she had to play an English duchess in one scene.

First she said I could stay with Grandad. But when she phoned Mum to tell her she said she didn't want me to be left alone with a man. Gene was furious and said, "What do you think he's going to do, Rita, eat her?" which made me larf so much I had to go out. They had a long fratch and Gene banged the phone down. Then Grandad said he couldn't look after me anyway, he had to work. So then Gene said she'd have a think. When she'd thought she said Alice how would you like to come to Spain with me?"

At first I was terribly excited. I'd only been abroad once before, when Gene took me to EuroDisney outside Paris when I was seven. Mum had to get me my own passport. EuroDisney was just so wonderful. I liked Casey Junior best and Thunder Mountain worst, but Thunder Mountain was what I remember most cos I was so scared and so was Gene, we just clung together and we both screamed our heads off as the train went like mad through the tunnels and we nearly fell out.

We stayed three days and did everything. I liked trying to pull the sword out of the stone and seeing the dragon in his cave and meeting Yasmin from "Aladdin". She shook hands with me. Gene did everything with me and we had a brilliant brilliant time.

But going to Spain was different. I was suddenly scared to leave Mum. I thought I might never come back. I kept remembering she'd said in her funny moods that she thought Gene wanted me for herself and might try to keep me. Gene was crazy about me (she often said "I love you to distraxion") so I thought it was <u>possible</u>. So I cried alot and wouldn't tell Gene why which drove her mad. She said ring Mummy and talk to her, so I phoned her (Gene never listened to my phone calls but anyway I took the cordless right down the garden). I thought Mummy would say come home, but she'd forgotten about Gene maybe stealing me and said I had to go to Spain. She said it's good for you to see other countrys and anyway I can't have you home just now because I'm job-hunting in London. She sent my passport in the post.

I still moaned a bit till Gene lost her temper and said you know I can't stand all this cattawalling and if you don't stop it I won't take you and you'll have to stay with Grandad and you know men don't know how to plat hair. I don't know why that made me larf, I could just imagine Grandad trying to do my pigtail and getting all tangled up and starting to swar.

So then we flew to Spain and strait away on the plane it was great because we had our own little TV screens with cartoons and they gave me a present (a bag with crayons and a pad – I did a good picture of Gene sitting beside me and of our meal). A huge car met us and took us to the hotel in Madrid. I'd never been in a real posh hotel before. The part where you go in, called the foyay, was like a palace. It had a glass roof and lots of lights. The floor was one huge carpet with patterns on it. There were sofas and chairs with stripy seats and huge tables with golden legs and glass tops and huge big vases of flowers nearly to the sealing like in a painting. And mirrors with gold frames all carved with fat babies and fruit.

When we got up to our room I couldn't believe it. We both had double beds!!! The carpet was so soft I wanted to lie on it. There was a view of the city through the window, you could see the lights just coming on. You pulled the curtains shut with a string. There was more furniture in the room than we had in our whole flat. The bathroom was just so shiny!

Gene put my suitcase on the bed and told me to unpack. I'd taken it from Brighton to Gene and Grandad's house full of my old ordinary clothes for the country. I opened it and nearly fell over. It was full of lovely new clothes!! I said to Gene, did you go shopping, and she said no they're Jessie's that she's grown out of, Marion gave them to you."

She picked out a black dress with white dots and a white collar and told me to put it on because we were going to have a posh dinner and I had to look nice. I don't wear dresses much and I didn't like it till I got it on and Gene buttoned it at the back and tied the sash and I looked at myself. I looked like someone else, like a rich girl in an old black and white movie.

Gene said, "You are a very pretty child," and I said "You're a very pretty old lady," and she said "oy, not so much of the old." But she was pretty with her blonde hair and lots of make up and her smart suit and lots and lots of silver stuff, necklaces and earrings and rings. She did my hair with a black velvit scrunchy band at the back instead of a plat, and put a tiny bit of her sent on my rists and said I was fit to be a duchess's grandaughter. The trouble was shoes, but she said my sandals would have to do and no one would see them under the table.

The dining room was grand like a palace there must of been about a hundred tables there all with pink table cloths and napkins that matched and loads of silver knives and forks and spoons and beautiful glasses. A waiter came and held my chair while I sat down. I was so nervous I was all trembly but Gene held my hand and said in her deepest voice, "Stick with me, kid," which is what she always said when we did anything new and I was scared.

The menus were huge cards and Gene read me what I could order but the food was funny. There was nothing really that I liked because most of it was red meat or strange things. I only like the food I'm used to and Gene always says I'm a fusspot and sometimes she's been really annoyed with me when I say I don't like things, but this night she was nice. She asked the waiter if he could bring me some spaghetti and grated cheese. She made me taste her food (she had three different things) she says I'm missing all the good tastes and that I must keep trying new things but I only liked the little potatoes, and afterwards there were some yellow soft sweet things that tasted like orange marzipan, and I did like those alot, but I liked my ice cream best.

I forgot to say that we weren't alone, there were some Spanish people at the table. Gene had taught me to say "Hola" which means hello and I said it to everyone and shook hands before we sat down. Then I was allowed just to eat while all the grown-ups talked in English with Spanish accents. I thought they were all actors but Gene said they were just people to do with making the film.

I was hoping and hoping that I'd be able to watch the filming but Gene said I couldn't because I'd be in the way, and that I was to have a minder. That night we slept in our double beds. I'd never slept in such a huge bed before and it was rather lonely. I hoped Gene would say I could cuddle in with her but she didn't. She said she had to get a good night's sleep because of filming in the morning. She went to bed the same time as I did!

Before it was even light someone knocking woke me up. While I was still half asleep a man came right into the room with a tray of coffee to help Gene wake up. Then we got dressed and then there was another knock on the door. Gene said it was my minder. Of course I thought it would be a woman so I nearly fell over when I opened it and outside was a man!!!

He was young and tall and had black shiny hair and a mustash. He was drop dead gorgeous like a movie star and I just staired at him and he smiled at me and bowed and put his hand out. I went to shake it but he kissed it! I felt terribly shy.

"Alice, this is One," she said. Later I found out you spell it Juan but I always think of him as One. I <u>knew</u>, I absolutely knew that Mum would go spare and ape and bananas if she knew I had a man minder, especially a young one, especially when Gene didn't even know him, but Gene just said "One will look after you. I'll see you this evening after work. Then she kissed me and waved to One and I was left alone with him.

I was <u>so scared</u>. I thought he was going to do sex to me strait away. One smiled at me and said with his

Spanish accent, "Alice, you are the same age as my little girl and I am going to take you to play with her."

Mummy's told me so often never to go with strange men no matter what they say to tempt you. I just didn't know what to do. I felt <u>frozen to the floor</u>!! But I thought I can't just stay in this bedroom all day and besides I was starving.

So I said in a kind of squeaky voice can we have breakfast first, and he said, "Of course. Shall we eat in the dining room? Somehow that made me feel better because nobody does sex to people in a dining room, so I kind of unfroze and we went down in the lift together where I suppose you <u>could</u>, but he didn't, and we went to the big dining room and the waiter pulled out my chair again and everything seemed normal even the breakfast which I chose from a long table that had everything you could ever want to eat for breakfast on it, except toast. But I had a crussant with jam in fact three (One had to cut them open for me cos they're so skwudgy my first one fell to bits).

So then we got in his car and drove through the streets for quite a long way and I was worried again, I began to think he was kidnaping me so I asked him, and he gave a big larf and said "If I did your

grandmother would kill me and I don't want to die."
I said my mother would kill you too and he said I
don't want to die <u>twice</u>."

After that I felt safe with him and anyway we got
to his house and his wife Inez was there and his little
girl. Her name sounded like One-eater. I started
larfing, I couldn't help it because I thought she might
as well be called "Eat-my-Dad" (like Bart Simpson
says "Eat my shorts"!!!). Later Gene wrote it for me,
it's Juanita.

Anyway the day with Juanita started really well,
we played in the garden in the morning, Juanita had
this great play-house made like a real house with
windows and a door with a key and there was like a
shop inside with a counter and shelves and lots of
little jars of real things like dried beans and
mackeroni in them and a scales and little bags and
we played shop all morning and I taught her the
English words for things and I learnt to say, "I want
some of those and how much in Spanish but I've
forgotten it now.

Juanita spoke quite alot of English and I was
surprised. They learn it at school. We've started
French but I couldn't speak to a French person. I
wondered how come Spanish kids learn English so

quickly. I asked Juanita and she said, "you must to learn English so that is why" which didn't make much sense.

Then we had lunch, a proper sitdown lunch with One and Inez, it was very funny ricey stuff called pieaya which was pretty, not a pie, more like a painting of food than something you eat. I didn't like to say I didn't like it so I ate some and I found I did like it (only not the musles which are really gross).

The day came to a bad end though which I don't like to think about. I'd better write it and get rid of it. Juanita told me about her little cousin who was coming to play in the afternoon. She pulled a face. When the cousin came I saw why. His name was Clowdio, he was younger than us and he didn't speak English and had a runny nose and he was an awful newsance so Juanita wispered to me let's do a trick. So we played hide-and-seek and when Clowdio hid in the play-house we sneaked up to it and locked him in with the key. The trick was Juanita's idea but if I have to tell the truth, he only hid in there because I told him to.

We only ment to leave him there for a bit so we could finish our game we'd been playing before he came (we'd stopped playing shop) but he was making noises and knocking so we went to the front garden where there was a good climing tree and we played "Gorillas in the Mist". She hadn't seen the film but Mum had the video and I told her about it. I was the big gorilla who creeps up and touches her hand.

Then One called us because Clowdio's mother had come to take him home. One said "Where's Clowdio?" and we looked at each other. It had been a long time since we locked him in the play-house and we'd forgotten all about him. Juanita said something in Spanish in a little mumbly voice and One and Inez rushed out into the garden and brought Clowdio in. He was all crying and histerical. I got a shock and so did Juanita I could see from her face which went all white.

Of course One couldn't tell me off much because I was a gest but Juanita really caught it. I was shocked again because her mother grabbed her and shook her and smacked her bottom hard twice, and then dragged her off upstairs. Clowdio's mother looked at me, a terrible cold look as if she'd like to kill me. She picked Clowdio up and carried him away.

Then I had to leave. On the way back to the hotel

in the car One asked "Well Alice was it you put it into Juanita's head to do something so cruel?" He was blaming me. I wanted to say that it was Juanita's idea but I didn't want to snitch because I could see they were a smacking family. But I felt very very horrible and I cried but he didn't say anything nice to make me feel better, like Mum mostly does if she's told me off and made me cry, he just took me into the hotel and sat with me in the foyay. He never said one more word.

I watched the big revolving doors until I saw Gene come in to the hotel. I was so scared One would snitch on me about Clowdio but he didn't. Gene was looking very tired and she didn't ask him anything, just thanked him and kissed me and took me up to our room. I didn't even say goodbye to One, I didn't get a chance because he just walked away.

I was determined not to cry or do anything that would make Gene ask me questions but she guessed something was wrong. She kept asking and in the end I told her. She sat with me on the bed with her arm around me and after a long time she said, "Well, darling, that was pretty mean all right, Clowdio was probably frightened in there, but sometimes one does things without thinking. I did something worse than that once." I asked what, and she told me she'd lost her temper and pushed <u>her</u> little cousin off the end of a jetty into a lake and he'd nearly drowned. She said "I used to get furious with him because he was such a little pest. But I loved him really and after that I knew I had to control my temper. I've got an awful temper, and that's something you haven't got. You just did what you did out of thoughtlessness and that's not as bad as doing it out of anger." After that I cried some more and she cuddled me and then I changed into another new Jess-dress and we went down for dinner.

This time there were no other people we had to eat with and Gene said, "That dining room's a bit toffee nosed. Would you like it better if we went out and found some little place? Maybe they've got something like Pinocchio's." All we could find was a McDonald's which I've never been in because I'm not allowed beef but I don't think Mum knows you can get chickenburgers. Gene eats beef, she says if she's going to get mad cow disease she caught it years ago so she had a half-pounder with double cheese and we got two big boxes of chips, and she said this is very bad for my figger." I forgot to say Gene is rather fat but she dresses to hide it.

I'm going to watch Oprah Winfry with Mum. I love her. Last week it was about men who beat up their wives. Mum switched off before the end cos those men made her sick but I saw most of it. Gene used to say Mum lets me watch unsuitable programmes. She said it was wrong for young children to watch grown-up programmes or rubbishy programmes. Gene thinks alot of what's on TV is junk and nearly all pop is junk and that was what the Big Row was about, well part of it. I'll write about that tomorrow. Right now I have to write a made-up story for Brandy. I'm going to be very careful of punctuation this time so she can't grumble and I'll get an A.

SCHOOL NOTEBOOK

THE MAGIC CARTOON

by Alice Williamson-Stone

Crystal was watching her favourite cartoon. It was The Simpsons. While she was larfing at it, there was a freeze-frame. Suddenly Bart Simpson stepped out of the TV leaving Lisa and Maggie moshunless on the screen.

"Hi, Crystal!" Bart said, and started to grow! He grew until he was as big as Crystal. But he was still yellow and he still had big round eyes and his hair still stuck up like a crown and he still had only four fingers. He said, "I've been wanting to visit England because I think I can do some serious damidge here. Only joking! Do you have a skateboard?" Crystal was so surprised she just shook her head. Bart said share mine and he produced it from behind his back.

They went out and Bart stepped on to his

skateboard and said jump on behind me. Then they started and it was just like at the beginning of the cartoon when Bart comes flying out of school and then crossing roads without looking and causing kayos. Crystal hung on to Bart's waist and let him do all the steering and it was the biggest fun she'd ever had. Everyone was stairing and jumping out of the way and a policeman chased them but he couldn't catch them and then they came to the river and Bart got up speed and then they just flew right across! They bounced once on the top of a barge that was going by.

When they landed on the other bank Bart stopped and said "now let's do something wicked." Crystal didn't much want to be wicked so she said "I wish Lisa was here" and Bart said "Lisa's a pain in the but, don't you like being with me?" Crystal said, "Yes, sorry, I loved the ride, what do you want to do?" Bart said, "Let's go bust in on the Queen." OK said Crystal, the palace is just up this main road.

So they zoomed along some more right over a traffic jam using the roofs of the red buses and bouncing off the cars and when they came to Buckingham Palace the guards started running around trying to stop them getting in but Bart just did a great big leap with his skateboard and they sailed right over the iyon fence. Bart maniged to snatch one of the guard's big fir hats off and put it on his head and it came right down to his shoulders! So he didn't see the Queen as she came rushing out of the palace to see what was happening and he ran right into her and knocked her flying, and Crystal and Bart went flying too and they all landed up in a heap.

The guards opened the big gates and surrounded them and pointed their rifles at Bart who said is there a problem officers? like Eddy Murphy in Trading Places. They tried to arrest Bart and Crystal but the Queen got up and said "You foolish men can't you see that this is the famous and fabulous Bart Simpson? Form a guard of honour!" So they stood in two lines and the Queen led them in between to the doors of the palace and she even made one guard carry Bart's skateboard in front of them on a cushon.

When they got inside Crystal wispered "Bart take your hat off it's rude to wear hats in the house" so Bart took off the fir hat and the queen gave a shreek and said, "Bart, you've got a crown just like me are you Royal?" and Bart said No mam that's just the way my hair grows. The Queen said, "I wish my hair grew like yours then I wouldn't have to wear the crown, it's so heavy it gives me a headake." And she asked them to stay for tea. Crystal was glad it was Bart and not Homer because Homer's table manners are so terrible but Bart ate quite nicely and when he reached too far for a cake Crystal nudged him and the queen passed it to him very gratiously.

After tea the Queen asked if they wanted to skateboard home or if they'd like a ride in her roles Roys. Bart said yes mam if I can ride on the roof and the Queen said that would be OK. So they drove back home with Crystal sitting beside the uniformed choffer and Bart balancing on his skateboard on the roof and shouting Hi there you poor Brits don't you wish you lived in Springfield USA! to the crowds. The crowds didn't like this and some of them threw things at him but he just caught the things and threw them back so it was a very exciting trip.

When they got back into the house Bart said "I gotta go now" and he climed back into the TV and the freeze-frame started moving again and Lisa said wherever have you <u>been</u> Bart and he said visiting the Queen of England and she said in your dreams! and just then I woke up it had all been in <u>my</u> dream but what a good dream it was.

Quite a good effort, Alice. Copy spellings 5 times
each: motionless, damaged, gracious, cushion,
Rolls Royce, shriek, iron, fur, chaos, chauffeur,
headache, managed.

B+.

Special ~~SCHOOL~~ PRIVATE NOTEBOOK

B plus! <u>B plus</u>! I just don't believe it. I worked half the night and tried my very very best. I read it to Nicola before school and she said it was <u>absolutely brilliant</u>. Mum thought so too when I read it to her on the train. She said it was my best story. And Brandy gives me a lousy rotten stinking B plus!

I wrote motionless out five times and damaged twice then I gave up. I'm not writing them out five times for <u>her</u>. Of course she <u>well</u> told me off but I was so cross I said, "Miss Brand I thought you gave me an unfair mark. It was a really good story." She said yes Alice it was. But A is for nearly perfect work and there were still alot of punctuation mistakes and I didn't like you ending it with "it was all a dream". Don't you hate stories that end like that? I hadn't thought about it, I was tired and I just wanted to end it, and Brandy said, exactly. It's a cop-out, Alice. If you're going to put magic into a story, make it real magic, that way we won't feel cheated. Oooh I <u>hate</u> her hate hate hate her. If Copper was here I'd get her to bite her. Only Copper's not like Lady, she doesn't bite people.

I want to write about the first letter. The one Mum censered.

One night soon after the Big Row we got home and there was a letter for me from Gene. I picked it up off the mat but Mum snatched it. She said she had to read it first. Mum has never even peeped into my letters (Gene used to write to me alot) and I threw a fit but she just said I have to Alice, I can't have her turning you against me. I said Gene wouldn't do that and she said "Oh wouldn't she." She went to her bedroom and bolted the door.

She was in there for ever. At first I stood and shouted through the door "Give me my letter, what about my privacy?" but she didn't come out and I got hungry so I went and had two choclate biscuits. When she came out she said there, and handed me a letter <u>in her handwriting</u>. I said what's this, and she said, "there were things in the letter I didn't want you to read so I've copied it out without those things." Mum is dead against censership in movies and books and I shouted, "You censered my letter!" and she said yes I did, now read it or don't and leave me alone, I've got enough to be upset about. And she went back into her room and bolted the door again and I could hear her crying.

I'll stick the letter Mum gave me in here.

My darling Alice,

Well, this is horrible, isn't it. It's a bit like when people get divorced. They always tell the children, "This is nothing to do with you, we love you just the same, we just can't get on with each other." This is true this time. Mummy and I can't get on and we're angry with each other but I still love you and of course Mummy is still your Number One which is the main thing. But I miss you a bunch and a bundle and a barrel and a heap. And one day maybe you and I will be able to see each other and in the meantime I'm still your grandma even if I can't be your Number Two.

Love forever, Gene

Well I knew when Mum copied it she must of left out most of it because when I picked it up from the hall mat before Mum snatched it I felt it was really thick and this was just one mouldy paragraph. It drives me crazy not knowing what she left out.

I waited for Mum to come out of her bedroom which she had to in the end because crying always makes her want to see TV. She walked strait to the set and turned it on and I turned it off and she turned it on. She said "Alice don't do that, I am not in the mood." I stood in front of the TV so she couldn't watch and started to nag her. What happened with Gene, why did you row with her, why aren't I going to see her any more? At first she just wouldn't say a word, not anything, but I kept on at her until she suddenly took hold of me and sat me down on the sofa. Actully she almost threw me, it was almost like Mrs Blewitt. "All right, she said, this is what happened.

You've heard Gene critisising me about the way I bring you up. She thinks I tell you things I shouldn't and that I've put you off men and I let you watch TV that's too grown-up for you and she thinks I take you to trashy movies and that I don't cook the right foods for you. And she thinks I'm a hypercondriak and I fuss too much about your health."

I said, "Well you did tell me that if a moskito bit me I'd get malaria, and that was silly." She said, "I didn't say that and don't call me silly Alice. The fact is Gene just can't mind her own business. I know she's done alot for you and I'm greatful but I can't let her tell me how to treat you or what to let you watch, that's a mother's job not a grandmother's."

I said yes, but that's been going on ever since she first came. Something else must have happened.

She said, you remember the night we spent at her new flat. I didn't want to be there and I was nervous and when you were asleep Gene and I started to talk and she suddenly said had I taken you to see Batman? We'd had a fratch about it ages ago, she said I shouldn't, but I told her I had and that it was none of her business. She said she was sick and tired of being the one who took you to all the good things like the ballet, and plays, and buying good books and good tapes for you, when all I did was feed you rubbish. She said if I didn't start backing her up about giving your mind the best instead of going against her she didn't see why she should spend thousands of pounds giving you a privalijed education. I think she was threatening to stop paying your fees."

Now to be truthful I hadn't liked Batman in fact I had nightmares about the Jester but I usually love going to the movies with Mum <u>specially</u> the grown-up ones. So I said, "but I like going to movies and watching TV with you just as much as going to plays and the ballet with Gene."

She said "I know and I think I'm giving you a balance so you can decide what's good and what's bad.

I said "Was that all?" Mum said no. The really bad part came later.

And when she said that, suddenly I knew what it was, because I was there in the room when it happened.

THE MAGIC SHOWER

by Alice Williamson-Stone

In my grandma's house is a magic shower. It works like this. You're in the bath and you've washed your hair and you need the shower to rinse out the shampoo. So this shower is a rubber hose that fits on to the taps so you turn on the water and mix it to the right tempratur and you start rinsing your hair and suddenly you're not in the bath any more you're in a pool on a dessert island and you're not holding a rubber pipe you're holding a snake!!!

And you try to let it go but it curls tight around your hand. And you are dead scared of course. But it's not a fierce snake. It curls round your hand in a friendly way until just its tail is holding you and then it begins to tug you to follow it.

It pulls you along until you come to some thick

jungle and you peep through and see a fancy dress party going on on the beech with a steel band. And you're very embarased because you haven't any clothes on because of being in the bath before the magic worked and you tell the snake you want to stay in the bushes and the snake hisses to some monkeys that come and bring some beautiful big shiny leaves and flowers and they fasen them on to you like a dress, they even put flowers in your hair.

Then the snake tugs you out into the open and all the party people turn and see you and they all go WOW. The snake slides up your arm and around your neck and hisses in your ear, "you have to dance and sing." And it gives you magic power and you dance Spanish like Carmen and sing "There's a café on the corner" and they all applord.

All except one person who is a man dressed as a woman who says, "You aren't one of us." He comes towards you and you beg the snake to save you but it can't and the man picks you up and throws you in the sea. And all your leaves and flowers fall off and you think you're going to drown but then you find yourself back in the bath with the water going cold. And the snake says "Wasn't that fun?" and goes back to being a rubber shower.

This is very strange and a bit disturbing, Alice. More like a dream than a story. But I think I must give you an A this time. Punctuation is much better. Copy 5 times: temperature, desert, beach, embarrassed, applaud.

<u>When in doubt use your dictionary</u>.

An A at last! And she didn't say a word about my cursive either. The other girls are beginning to notice how I write and say it's nicer than theirs. We're at the doctor's. Mum's in with him having a check up and I'm writing this while I wait for her, I brought my special notebook with me.

The bad part happened not that night Mum was talking about but the next night. It was the night before I started at my new London school that Mum finally found for me but I think Gene got me in there at the last minute. She's quite famous and maybe that's why I passed the entrance test even though my maths are bad. My English is very good and I must say that's a bit because of Gene. She drove me crazy last summer making me do reading and comprehension tests all the time, she kept saying "read the rubric! read the rubric! Which ment the instructions and that really helped with the entrance test.

Mum had to take a day off work to take me to the uniform shop and Gene paid, she said it was a racket because you have to have a uniform and there's only one shop you can buy it at so they can charge what they like. Even the knickers cost a fortune and you have to have them for gym. She wouldn't pay for the blazer which was over £60 she said I could get a second-hand one at school but she bought the rest except walking shoes, Mum bought those. It was mostly dark grey but the blouse and sweater (and the blazer) were red and it looked really smart. I wished I could have a new blazer and I nagged but Gene said NO. She gets very stubborn if she thinks she's being ripped off.

Mum took everything to Gene's new flat and I put it on and showed off to Gene, and Mum and I slept there in her spare room which was all blue and lovely and had a lovely print by Klimpt who's our favourite. The next day was the day before my first day at school. That must of been the night they had that row Mum told me about. Anyhow Mum went off to work without saying much and I slept late and then Gene and I spent the day together.

She took me to Kew Gardens and we sat by the lake and played The Game (that's what actors call it) where you act out titles. I'm very bad at guessing but good at the acting. I wanted to act titles all the time and not have to guess but so did Gene. So we stopped playing and fed the ducks and swans and talked about religion.

Gene told me long ago she doesn't believe in God. But she said in the new school there would be prayers and alot of religious lessons because it's that kind of school and it would be best if I just listened at first and made up my own mind, but not to let anyone brain wash me. She said "Christian schools are often very good but that doesn't mean you have to believe things that don't make sense to you." She said asking questions was very important and that in good schools they want you to, even about God.

I always liked it the way Gene talked to me like a grown-up and I asked her about sex. She said I shouldn't get hung up about it because it's very nice when you really love someone. She said not all men are awful and predertery (that's like birds of pray and foxes). She said "Most people are kind and decent. You just have to learn to reconise the few bad ones which isn't easy but don't go being frightened of everyone, it'll spoil your life."

I said "Do you think my mum is frightened of

everyone?" and she said "Your mum has had a very difficult life and she's overcome a lot of hard things. She's done very well and you should be proud of her. But the hard things have made her suspishous and nervous. I hope your life will be easier and better and won't put you off people." I said, "Mum's my Number One and you're my Number Two." And she sat with her arm round me and we looked out over the water that was all glittery like flat fireworks and she said, "You're my Number Two too." I said, "What about Grandad?" and she said, "He and your dad are a tie for my Number One. But you're very close behind. I always wanted a little girl and although I wish some things were different I love you to distraxion."

Then we went back to our house. She'd bought special sandwiches and cream donuts which she adors but which make her feel guilty and we had tea. Then we rehearsed a play for about an hour with the cut-out toy theatre Gene made for me ages ago after she took me to the Toy Theatre Museum. It was a mellowdrama called Maria Martin in the Red Barn, which was so funny, Gene did the villun with a mad larf and I did Maria. I had to do her lines while I moved the little cut-out figgers on a wire. Maria on a wire, it rhymes.

When Mum came home from work we made her sit down and we did the play for her. I didn't even have to read my part, I knew it already, and I did Maria screaming as she was being chased by the villun, and I did the hero too who came to rescu her with a deep voice. We got our wires in a bit of a tangle but it went really well. Mum looked very tired and I was disappointed because she didn't get excited about our play she just got up and said, "Very good, now I need my tea." (Mum always says she's a tea-aholic. I wished I'd saved a cream donut for her.)

She said I had to go to bed early because of school which was a long journey away on the train and a bus but I hadn't had any supper and we had nothing much in the house so Gene said she'd go out and buy us all an Indian take-away which is my favourite. So she went out.

And while she was out the phone rang and it was Marion, Gene's friend in the country, the one with the ponies. I don't know why she phoned, perhaps she'd forgotten Gene had moved to the new flat, anyway I suppose she asked Mum how she was, and suddenly I heard Mum spouting a whole bunch of stuff about Gene!! How she was interfering and then she said, "She is so egotistical and so aragant, she thinks because she's got money she can boss everyone about and get her own way, she can even tell me how to bring up my own child."

I couldn't believe it. She was getting really worked up, she was really furious. I kept tugging her and shaking my head. Because Marion was Gene's friend, and I knew Mum shouldn't be slagging Gene off to her. But Mum just seemed to go a bit crazy and I couldn't stop her. Then I couldn't believe it even more, she started asking Marion if she thought Gene looked after me properly when I'd been staying with her!! She said "I never had an easy moment when she was away from me." And then we heard Gene at the front door and Mum said goodbye quickly to Marion and hung up.

Gene came in with the food and said, "Hey, nobody's laid a table!" so I ran to do it and Mum just sat there as if she was zonked out. She does this sometimes when she's upset she sort of goes away, she calls it withdrawing. It's like hiding from everyone even though she's still there. Gene opened all the little boxes full of lovely Indian food all red and shiny in foil boxes and stuck spoons in them and I put the plates and glasses of water and knives and forks on the table but Mum sat at the dark end of the room and wouldn't come to eat. I felt scared and went to wisper to her to come but she pushed me away and said "I'm not hungry" in her funny voice.

So Gene and I ate together. Gene knew something was wrong but she didn't know what and afterwards she just said goodbye and good luck for school and left. I expect she kissed me but I can't remember it. I wish I could remember because that's the last time I saw her.

Writing all that at the doctor's gave me a question to ask Mum so I did on the bus. I said, "did Marion tell Gene what you said about her, was that what made her leave us?" and Mum got really annoyed with me. She said "Why don't you ask me what the doctor said instead of banging on all the time about that bloody woman. I went quiet because I hate it when Mum talks crossly to me in public and I had hurt feelings. But when we got home I got worried and said what did the doctor say. She said she had to have some tests but the doctor thinks she's got an illness.

I felt myself go all funny inside as if I might faint or something. I started crying and I said it's not canser is it because a girl's mother at school died of canser in Brighton. She said no nothing so bad but it's something that makes your joints ake and makes lumps come out on your neck. You don't die from it but it makes you feel rotten and all I need right now with the house and the job and everything is more trouble with my health.

Mum started to cry too and I put my arms round her but I was thinking, if Gene knew about this she might come back and help us or at least let us stay in the house. But I didn't dare say anything, I knew Mum would go crazy because she's very proud. I mean if she'd never go back to Liverpool or ask for help even from her own mum because she thought she hadn't been on her side against the Big Pig, of course she wouldn't ask Gene for help now she's That Bloody Woman. I'm still on Mum's side 110% but I know she shouldn't of lost it and slagged off Gene to Marion. Gene must of been so hurt when she heard what Mum'd said.

I told Nicola and Alexandra at school about Mum's illness. But I couldn't talk about Gene at school. Mum had told me not to and anyway I couldn't. But I needed to talk to someone so today when I was at Sharon's I told Peony. Peony hasn't got a grandma and she's only eight so I didn't really expect her to be much use but she said, "let's play, and I'll be you and you be Gene."

I put on a dress of Sharon's and Sharon pinned my hair up and lent me a hat, not that Gene wears hats but to be grown-up, and Peony put on my blazer. (I got a second-hand one.) Strait away Peony got really angry (pretend) and said, "Why did you leave us and be so horrible and make my mum hate you and want to throw us out?" I started to say about giving the house to my dad, but Peony interrupted. She said "I know all that but it's no excuse. You're my grandma and you're supposed to love me and look after me, that's what grandmas do."

Somehow I didn't like her being so mean to Gene. I said "How do you know, you haven't even got one." Peony said, "You're being you, not Gene, be Gene and answer." So I said, "I do love you but I can't manage with your mum. She just exployted me. She even thinks I didn't look after you in the country and I did. If I can't see her I can't see you."

I was already a bit shocked to hear myself saying all that, specially about Mum exployting her. But then I got another shock because Peony stopped being me and started crying which I'd never seen. She took off my blazer and threw it on the floor and shut herself in her bedroom. After I coxed her through the door, she finally said, "You said what my dad said to me, that he couldn't see me without my mum and he couldn't stand her. He's rotten and so is your grandma. If they loved us it wouldn't matter if they didn't like our mums." I said, "My mum had a big row with my grandma." Peony said, "My dad and mum fort all the time, but so what. If he loved me he wouldn't care." She was saying Gene didn't love me, or not enough. That really hurt and we both got a sad mood and didn't play any more.

Today after assembly Brandy said Mrs Dev wanted to see me. I made a face and said gulp what for and Brandy said, "Don't dramatise Alice, just trot along. So I troted along but I wasn't exactly happy I mean like what could the headmistress want me for? You usually only have to go to her office if you've done something.

Mrs Dev made me sit down and said "Miss Brand told me your grandmother died, Alice, but she hasn't died has she? I saw her on a panel on television last night." I said what panel? I was <u>astonished</u>. I've seen Gene on TV alot, but never on a panel where it's live. Mrs Dev told me what it was but I'd never heard of it.

I wished and wished I'd seen it, it would of been like seeing her again.

She said why did you tell Miss Brand she'd died? I said I didn't. She said well Miss Brand said you looked very sad when she asked and you didn't answer so she thought she had died. I sort of mumbled something. She gave me a funny look and said, "Listen Alice, I'd like to invite your grandmother to be our special gest at prize giving. We like to invite someone from the media specially if it's a relative of one of our girls. Would you like it if she came and gave the prizes?"

I didn't know what to say. It was sort of a shock. I'd of loved it before the Big Row. I'd of been so proud. But that was then. Now everything was different and horrible and I got that pain again.

Mrs Dev waited and then said, "You don't have to ask her, I will. I just wanted to know if you had any objexions." I shook my head. She said are you all right, Alice, you've gone rather pale. I said I was OK. But really I wasn't because my head shake ment no, don't ask her, please don't.

Luckily prize giving isn't until June. Maybe she won't be able to come. I know Mum would die if she knew Gene was coming to our school.

The other night we watched a film on TV about a family in Ireland long ago that was evicted. The landlord came on a horse with some people called bailifs and threw them out. I couldn't sleep after it. The kids were all dirty and crying and it was <u>horrible</u>. I asked Mum if that could happen to us and she said "No. We've still got our flat in Brighton, I'll never let us be homeless," so then I felt better. Of course, Gene knows we've got the flat in Brighton so she's not really like that landlord.

I keep asking Mum every day if she's found somewhere. I know she hasn't. I don't think she's even looking. Of course it's hard to flat-hunt when you haven't got a car and when you're working. Gene once offered Mum driving lessons for her birthday but Mum didn't want to. Now she says this illness she has might mean she wouldn't be allowed to drive. She akes and has to sit down alot. She's supposed to rest but she can't. She can't even tell her bosses at the practiss about the illness because they might fire her. She has pills for the illness but sometimes she forgets to take them. I have to remind her.

Mum really is a bit of a hypercondriak, but it's about me. That's her big thing, worrying I'll get ill. If I get a headake she thinks its mygrain and if I have tummy ake she thinks it's ecoli or legionaires disease. She always told me not to let anyone kiss a cut better because of aids. I wouldn't even let Gene and when I told her she might give me aids she just went WHAAAAT!

I have to write a story for Brandy about a wicked witch. I wish it was about a wicked landlord, then I could write about Gene riding a big horse and coming to our street with the bailifs. I'm going to do a drawing of her. I have this magic idea that if I draw things I'm scared of carefully I won't be scared any more. I don't want to be scared of Gene.

THE BAD REWARD

by Alice Williamson-Stone

Jack was a girl of ten. Her real name was Jacqueline. She wore boys clothes and was very brave, she wasn't afraid of anything at all. All the bullies in her school ran away when she arrived on the scene. Sometimes she rescued other children who were being bullied so they all respected her.

One day she was walking home from school alone (she was allowed to because she was so strong nobody would dare hurt her) she saw an old fat lady trying to cross the road not at the crossing. She said,

"You shouldn't cross except at the crossing madam."

The fat old lady said,

"But I have to cross here my legs are bad and I can't walk any further" so Jack stepped out in the road and put her hands up and stopped all the cars and the old lady crossed. Then the old lady said,

"That was foolish but very brave. I like it when children do brave and foolish things to help me. I would like to give you a special reward." She gave Jack a strange very small machine with a handle. The old lady said,

"When you have any problem turn the handle." Then she vanished. That same day Jack had a problem with her maths homework, she couldn't do it, so she turned the handle. She almost dropped the machine with fright because it played a loud tune! But when Jack looked at her maths book the sum was all done. In fact all her homework was done.

The next day at school her teacher said,

"Jack your sums are all right. Can you show me how you worked them out?" Jack had no idea and the teacher said "I think your parents did the homework. That's cheating. I give you a big F and you will have to go to the Head's office." Outside that office Jack thought "This is a big problem" so she took out the

machine and turned the handle. It played another loud tune and there was a BANG from inside the office. Jack peeped in and saw that the Headmistress had gone mad, she was pointing a gun at the door and saying, "Get out or I'll shoot you!" Now Jack knew that the old lady had been a witch and that the magic music machine only helped in a bad way so she threw the machine away in the dustbin. But next day she heard a loud tune in the next classroom and then someone shouted "Fire!" and everyone started running. The school burnt down. Then Jack knew some other child had found the witch's machine and that the bad magic could go on for ever.

A. Not a single spelling mistake! But what a sinister story! You do write very well I must say. In a weird kind of way! See me after school.

Special ~~SCHOOL~~ PRIVATE NOTEBOOK

Brandy told me there's a creative writing competition she wants me to enter. She said handwriting counts and she wants me to do joined-up-print like the others. I said can I use a word processer but she said no. "Now make it a nice story, not one of your strange sinister ones. And it has to be at least 350 words long. And no drawings, just the story (because I often ilustrate my stories)." That sounded alot but when I counted my last story about the witch it was 452 words long! So the only problem will be, keeping it nice enough. (Gene said nice was a silly flabby word. I don't want to write nice stories, I like sinister ones better.)

Mum didn't go to work this morning. Her illness made her feel too bad. I am really worried about this illness. I wish I could talk to Gene about it. I keep thinking about phoning her and just telling her Mum has this illness which is called sarcoidosis. The trouble with having only a Number One is that if there's something wrong with her you don't have any other number to talk to.

So then I had my idea. I thought "I have a Number Three, sort of." I decided to phone my Auntie Carla.

Mum had to get up and come and fetch me from Sharon's. What would happen if she <u>couldn't</u> get up? She often says a single parent can't be ill. It's a long journey with lots of waiting for buses and stuff and she looked really rough and she walked like an old person because of her joints. As soon as we got home she said "I'm sorry Alice you'll have to get your own tea, I must go to bed." As soon as she was asleep I shut her door very quietly and went downstairs and looked for Auntie Carla in Mum's adress book. I felt sneaky because I knew Mum wouldn't let me but I felt so lonely I had to.

I asked her how she was and how baby James was and then she asked me why I was phoning. I said "Mum's ill with sarcoidosis." She asked what it was and I explained. She said "I'm really sorry, but what can I do, Alice, I'm in Liverpool and you're in London." I said "Somebody's got to help us." And then I heard myself say, "What about your mum?" (who is Mum's mum too). I felt my head go all fuzzy when I heard myself say that, I hadn't ment to, it just came out because I was thinking grandmothers. Auntie Carla said, "I could ask her." I said very quickly "But don't let Jonas know." Jonas is the Big Pig's real name. I was so worked up I nearly said Big Pig!!

Auntie Carla asked for our new adress and phone number and that was it. Now I'm writing this to talk to myself. I am piling up secrets. It's easy for Mum to say secrets are bad. I can't tell her everything but if I don't I have this terrible pain inside, worse than about Gene. It bothers me all the time. I suppose it's my conshuns. I wonder what Peony does about hers. Maybe she hasn't got one. If I went on the rob I would have such a bad conshuns I don't know how I'd stand it. But what if Mum gets really too ill to take me to school and can't go shopping? I might have to go on the rob then.

Gene told me that when she was a child she walked to school by herself and very little kids went to the shops for their parents all the time and some people didn't lock their doors even at night. I wish it was still like that. Peony is bad in a way but she doesn't hurt anyone. I've never met anyone who hurts people (unless the prowler wanted to). Maybe it's just Mum being too afraid for me like Gene said. Maybe I could go to the shops by myself. I'm allowed to play out if I stay where Mum can see me. Ali's shop is just up the road. What can happen to me between here and there? Nothing happened to Peony and me for two hours in the streets near school and that's a bad district.

I've thought about it very hard and I'm going to buy stuff and make dinner for me and Mum.

Later. I did it. I did it! I went to Ali's all by myself with money from my moneybox and bought some Smash and a big tin of baked beans and a sliced lofe and some satsoomas. No one took any notice of me! I even crossed the main road by myself. Of course I was careful. It wasn't hard. You'd have to be <u>stupid</u> not to wait till there were no cars.

Still I was scared. Peony would larf her head off if she knew how dead scared I was. I ran all the way back with the shopping. I haven't got a key so I had left the door a little bit open. When I got in I almost fell on the floor, in fact I did but it was acting.

I got up and went to the kitchen and put the whistling kettle on. Gene gave Mum an electric one but she won't use it now and I couldn't find it. I hope she hasn't thrown it out. I poured the Smash into a bowl and when the kettle whistled I poured the boiling water and mixed with a fork. Then I put some butter in and tried to get the lumps out. I put some toast in the toaster.

Then I tried to open the tin of baked beans. I've never used the tin opener before and it's an old kind of one and I couldn't do it. So I thought now what do I do, and I thought, I'll ask next door. Next door are Julie and Matt our neighbours and they're nice. So I knocked and Matt came and opened the tin for me. He said "Are you cooking tonight Alice? Mum's not ill is she?" I wanted to say yes but I said no, I don't know why, I didn't want him to come in. I wanted to manage by myself. But it was nice to think that Matt was there.

In the end Mum woke up and came down just as I was putting the mashed potato and baked beans and toast on the table. I'd picked some flowers from the garden and lit a candle. She staired at it and said "Good God Alice how did you do all this?" I said "I took money from my moneybox and I went to Ali's cos there was nothing for supper."

Mum gave me this funny look as if she'd never seen me before and sat down at the table. I thought she would give me a real telling off but she didn't say a word. She ate supper and we had satsoomas for desert. She said did you boil the kettle and everything, and I said yes. She's never let me pick up the whistling kettle because the handle gets hot but I used the dishtowel like she does. Then she said "so could you make me a cup of tea do you think?" And I said "Mum I'm nine and three quaters. Peony can cook spaghetti and make tea and she's only 8. She makes the sorce too."

I turned around and went into the kitchen. Gene would of said, "Good exit." I felt great. Not about Mum being ill of course she really looked bad. But I thought I might not have to go on the rob and I can be more independant. But I still have a very bad conshuns about ringing Auntie Carla. I don't know

WHAT Mum is going to say if HER mum turns up. I'll have to worn her but I don't know how. I'm so tired I'm going to bed early. (I did all the washing up too.)

I thought Mum was better this morning but she was white and when we got to the station and the train was nearly coming she suddenly said "Could you go to school on your own Alice?" I was <u>frozen</u> to the <u>spot</u>. I said NO. She said, "All right let's go home then and you'll have to miss school because I just can't face that journey, I hurt too much."

It was our class day trip to the National Gallery so I really wanted to go to school so I said "Can I get a taxi to school from the train station?" We did that once instead of the bus when we were late so I knew where to wait in the queue. She thought about it and said "I suppose I'll have to let you but I'll be sick with worry all day." She gave me some money and said "Now don't talk to anyone, not anyone at all, do you understand? And keep your purse in your inside blazer pocket. Phone me when you get to school."

The train came in and I said how will I get home and she said don't worry, I'll think of something, and she kissed me and pushed me on to the train. I <u>know</u> she wouldn't of let me go if she hadn't been feeling really week and ill.

I was so worried about her and about Auntie Carla and maybe my other grandmother turning up that I wasn't even very scared of being on the train by myself. It was just like every day except I had to think more. Standing in the queue for the taxi outside the station was exciting. When it was my turn I told the taxi man the street of the school. I sat well back for safety and comfort like the notice says. The taxi man was very nice and talked to me but I didn't dare answer, he probably thought I was a real dumbo.

I phoned Mum from the school office. She said "Good girl, you're wonderful, now I can go to sleep." I told Mrs Dev she was ill and I'd come to school on my own and she was shocked and said, "All that way, how will you get home Alice and I said I didn't know. She said I think I'd better drive you. I said I could manage from Waterloo station because our station is just at the end of our road, and she said, "All right, that's on my way." I was releeved. Then I said, "Did you ask my grandma to do prize giving" and she said, all smily, "Yes and she's coming! We're all so pleased." I wasn't pleased and I wasn't not pleased, I didn't know how I felt, it was just something else to worry about.

SCHOOL NOTEBOOK

THE VISIT
TO THE NATIONAL GALLERY

by Alice Williamson-Stone

Today our class visited the National Gallery in Trafalgar Square. It was very good only I'd been before with my grandmother. That time I could only notice the clothes. The painted clothes were so wonderful velvits and satins and fur with every little fur hair painted I couldn't notice the faces much but my grandmother told me some of the stories of the pictures. I liked the aligories best because they had the best stories and I hated the hunting ones with all dead animals and birds even if the painting was very good, but we didn't do them today.

Miss Brand made us sit on the floor in front of some of the pictures and notice things. One picture showed <u>alot</u> of wild people beside the sea and Miss B said, "where do you think they're coming from" and Tanya said "Down the pub" and we all larfed but she was sort of right, they had been to a party and some of them were drunk like one old very fat naked man on a donkey and one with a big snake around him (I don't know why and nor did Miss Brand).

A different naked man was jumping out of a chariot with vine leaves in his hair. He was going to grab a dressed woman who was waving to a ship far out on the sea carrying her boy friend away so she wasn't interested in the naked one. There were <u>alot</u> of naked people in the pictures. We thought it was funny that the naked women showed everything but the naked men didn't. My grandma said that's because the painters were all men and they're shyer about their private bits. They do on statues though.

What a lot of emphasis on nakedness! That's not what's important! You didn't mention that that picture was based on the Greek myth of Bacchus and Ariadne. Don't write "a lot" as one word!

B.

Well, it wasn't worth much more than a B this time. Honestly I wasn't concentrating. Mrs Dev drove me to Waterloo and saw me on to the train. She said she'd tried to phone Mum at work and at home and couldn't get her and I said "She's in bed" but when I got to our house there was no answer when I rang the bell.

I knocked on Julie and Matt's door and Julie came and then I got a real shock because she said, "Come in Alice, your grandmother is here. I saw her waiting in the street so I asked her in." I started shaking. Could she mean Gene?

I walked in to Julie's living room and there was an old lady I'd never seen before and of course it was Mum's mum. She put out her arms and I had to go and be hugged. She held me a long time and I could feel she was trembling inside like trying not to cry. She held me away and looked at me with alot of tears in her eyes and said "I'm your nan." I knew Nan wasn't her name (her name is Doreen) but I'd heard kids at my first school calling their grandmothers nan. I said "Mum doesn't know you're coming. She gave a big sniff and said "Oh dear, that's very bad. What will she say?" I said "I don't know." I felt really frightened and terribly shy.

Anyway Julie made tea for us and you could see she was curious about why we didn't know each other and I got more and more scared but Nan talked to me and made me sit beside her and every now and then she hugged me and cried again. I felt really strange with her, she was so different from Gene, she talked with a funny accent and she had white hair (Gene dies hers blonde). She didn't look anything like Mum, well maybe a bit, but she was too old to notice it. Her clothes were old fashioned and not smart or ethnic like Gene's. She wore sent but that wasn't like Gene's either.

After for ever, Julie said "I think your mother is here (she was looking out of the window). I jumped up and started to shake again. I told Nan to wait while I told Mum and I went out and there was Mum just unlocking our front door. She looked a bit crazy and when she saw me she kind of screamed and grabbed me and shook me which she never does and said "Where the hell were you, I went all the way to Sharon's and she said you weren't at school."

I'd forgotten all about Sharon! I told her Mrs Dev drove me to the station and she said "Why didn't the stupid woman let me know?" I said she tried but you'd left. Then she hugged me and bursed into tears. I thought this was my worst ever moment because I had to tell her and I thought she'd go completely spare on top of how spare she was already.

We went into our house and Mum switched the lights on and said "I must have some tea, I feel like death." She went into the kitchen. I stood in the doorway and my mouth was all dry and I <u>made</u> myself say "Mum someone's come to see you, she's at Julie and Matt's." She stopped and looked at me. She said "What's wrong with you, you look worse than I feel." I said, "It's Nan, I mean it's Doreen, I mean it's your mum."

Her face went all twisted, not just white – like a stranger. She staired at me and said, "You sent for her." I just nodded. She said very quietly, "How could you Alice, you know how I feel." I said "I know but I got scared. You're ill and I might have to leave school and go on the rob." She said on the what, I said "stealing". Her mouth kind of dropped open.

The gas was coming out and she'd forgotten to light it so I took the gas lighter away from her and lit the gas which went BANG and we both jumped. Mum just stood there. Then suddenly she went out through the living room and out of the front door and I heard her knocking next door. I stood and watched the kettle and when it boiled I put two tea bags in our best mugs and made the tea and in a couple of minutes Mum and Nan came in. I can't write any more tonight.

Next morning. I'm on the train. Mum is sitting not next to me, she's across the ile. She's coming with me but she's not speaking to me.

Before she stopped speaking to me she said, "I have to accept what you did because it's done now. But I'm still very angry. I can't bear all this interference as if I was a child. It hasn't helped it's just made things worse. Today I'll take you to school but we're going to pretend I'm not here. First because I don't want to talk to you just now. Second because I want to see how you'd manage if I wasn't with you. Do what we always do. Don't get a taxi this time." I said "You mean catch the bus and walk from the bus stop to school?" It's ten minutes from the bus stop but no main roads to cross. She said yes. I'll follow you." I said "Can I come home alone and not wait for Sharon" and she said "no, I'm not turning you into a latchkey child. Not yet." I said "Are you well enough to go to work and she said who the hell cares if I'm well enough. I have to go and I have to pick you up afterwards." So now she's sitting across the ile reading the Times and pretending not to know me.

I didn't see Nan this morning. She slept in Mum's room and Mum slept on the sofa. I didn't hear anything they said last night because as soon as they came in from Julie's Mum sent me to my room and said "Do your homework and go to bed." Nan said "oh let the child stay Rita" and Mum turned on her and said in a fierce voice, "Mind your own business, Mother!" She wasn't going to let her start being bossy like Gene!! It was only six o'clock or something. I crept out later to the top of the stairs to listen but Mum heard me and shouted at me "Alice go to your room!" So I just wrote in my private book. I didn't do my homework, I couldn't. Brandy will kill me but I'll just tell her we had a family crysis.

The pain from my conshuns is better. Now I've got a new pain which is Mum being angry and not talking but it's not as bad as the conshuns. She can't keep it up. She'll have to start talking to me and if she doesn't I've got Nan to talk to.

THE CONSHUNS OF BACCHUS

by Alice Williamson-Stone

Bacchus went to a party one day with <u>alot</u> of his friends. Bacchus was the son of Zeus chief of the gods and that made him a bit of a huligan. There was <u>alot</u> to drink mostly wine which Bacchus was the god of.

Wine is made from grapes and so Bacchus wore vine leaves round his head of curly hair. Everyone loved him because he was so young and good looking and his wine made people feel better and forget their troubles.

After the party they all came through some woods. They were drunk and singing and one old drunk man fell off his donkey and everyone larfed (he wasn't hurt). Suddenly Bacchus saw a woman standing on the beach waving. She was so beautiful he wanted to marry her strait away. He jumped out of his chariot and seezed her in his arms. "I want to marry you" he said. "What is your name?"

She said "My name is Ariadne I can't marry you. Do you see that ship on the harizon? My sweetheart Theseus is on it. He's left me here on this horrible island, and after I saved his life."

Bacchus made everyone sit down and told Ariadne to tell them the story how she saved Theseus from the horrible minator so she did, but she was crying all the time. "How could he leave me?" she sobbed. "Without me and my idea for tying a thread and following it out of the maze he'd of been killed by the horrible minator." Everyone thought Theseus was a big pig and Bacchus kissed Ariadne and said,

"Forget him and marry me." So she did (marry him) but she never forgot Theseus and they were not very happy except when they were drinking lots of wine.

This is lovely, Alice, it made me laugh – was I meant to? But why did you call it "Conscience of Bacchus" – surely it was Theseus who should have had a bad conscience. Please don't write "of" when it should be "have", as in "would have" and "he'd have". AND DON'T WRITE "A LOT" AS ONE WORD!!! Write conscience, straight, seized, horizon, hooligan, laughed, Minotaur, and <u>he'd have been killed</u> 5 times each. Oh, all right then, 3 times each.

A–, despite the bad spelling! (This will <u>not</u> do for the competition because it's not exactly an original story.)

We've moved.

It happened quicker than Mum wanted it to. She had decided not to let Gene chase her out of Dad's house or at least make her go to alot of trouble. But it didn't happen. What happened was, Mum got a phone call from Dad's wife in Holland. Her name's Johanna. She said she was coming to England on a trip and she wanted to stay in the house!!! Mum said "where will you sleep" and she said, "anywhere, on the sofa if I must. But please don't expect me to go to a hotel when we have a house of our own."

Mum was in a terrible mood about this, angry and depressed both at once. She said it was a ploy which means a trick. She was withdrawn for two days (she was talking to me by then of course), but when she got calm she said she couldn't stay in the house with Dad's wife. I said why don't you lock her out and Mum said that would be breaking the law.

Mum got Nan to mind me all over two weekends

and Mum house-hunted I mean flat-hunted. We wanted a house but we couldn't afford it. In the end Mum got desprit and took this flat. It's only got one bedroom and the rooms are very small. And it's on the third floor. We're only renting it, not buying a place of our own which Mum wanted to.

She gave up the Brighton flat and got a van to bring all our things to here. So at least I got my own bed and my hammock (only I can't hang it up because the sealings are too week) and my toy animals and my old armchair and the big book case Gene bought me years ago. And all my books and games and puzzles but some of them seem a bit babyish now. And they make everything crowded cos Mum and me have to share. And the living room's long and narrow and there's no fireplace. (We had a gas fireplace in Gene's house and we used to light it on cold nights and cuddle up to it. Now we just have to cuddle up to the TV.) It feels so <u>small</u> after Gene's whole house. It's like Copper trying to curl up in Lady's basket!

Of course this means Nan couldn't stay but anyway she had to get back to Liverpool and the Big Pig. Me getting her to come turned out OK in the end even if it made Mum furious at first. She was very useful and I think her and Mum are not such bad friends now. I asked Mum if she'd talked about the Big Pig and how her mum hadn't helped her against him but she said no there was no point. She said her mum had limitations, there were things she couldn't do and it was no good expecting it. I said, "What things?" and she said, "Well she has some funny ideas like you have to put your man first and do what he tells you even if he's the most horrible person on earth." I know Mum would never think that, she would never do what some man told her.

And I sort of got another grandma. She couldn't do make up plays and sing and stuff like Gene did and certainly nothing sporty, but she was kind and never strict (Gene could be a bit strict when I food-fussed or cattawalled) and when she was here she watched lots of lovely rubbish programmes on TV and cooked us meals. It was great to have proper fried suppers every night with puddings. I even got to like rice pudding and bread-and-butter pudding. I never got to like cabbage though but at least that was the only vegtable Nan cooked, Gene had whole meals of vegtables. She taught me to cook lots of things so now I cook supper sometimes in our new kitchen. I can bake rock cakes too.

There's one good thing about the flat, it's just round the corner from school. So we don't need Sharon any more so now I only see her and Peony sometimes in the local shops (I always look for bumps in Peony's sweater to see if she's been on the rob). Now I'm a latchkey child. Mum's given me my own key on a ribbon round my neck and I walk home by myself and then lock myself in and get my own tea and stay alone till Mum gets back from work. It's about three hours most days.

I <u>hated</u> it at first and I sulked alot and Mum felt guilty but not having Sharon saves money. I wish I knew why we have to save so hard. I only get £1.50 pocket money a week. Alexandra and Nicola, and Sarah, AND Emma, all get £4. So anyway I just sat in front of the TV at first (I wouldn't do homework till Mum got back) but I got bored so I started reading all my old books and some of them are still good, the ones Mum used to read me, the Greek myths and some Australian Songlines ones, and the Jungle Book and some other good ones Gene gave me (like Wind in the Willows, but that's hard). When I get fed up reading I do alot of writing, stories and stuff, and drawing. But I do get lonely.

Mum said I am more independant now but I don't feel it. I still can't go out on my own except just to walk from school and even then Mum worries I will be kidnaped or molested (that means something bad men do, I'm not sure what). She still takes me to school every day.

THE MAGIC CACTUS

by Alice Williamson-Stone

When we moved into our flat there was nothing there at all except one thing. It was a cactus on our bathroom window ledge in a tin cup. It was droopy so I watered it and in a week it made three baby cactuses growing out of its sides. All green and prickly. One day I saw that one of them had a face. I thought I was imagining it but when I was cleaning my teeth I heard a tiny voice. It said, "Hello Jenny (that's my name by the way). I'm here because you saved my mum so I will give you a wish." I said, "I wish for ten more wishes" but when I said that, the baby cactus made a prickly face and yelled "Greedy" in his little cactus voice, and shriveled up.

When the next little cactus grew a face and spoke to me I said "I wish our flat was bigger and had a nice view over a park." The little cactus shouted "That's a ploy, you're trying to get two wishes so you won't get any wish at all!" And he shrank up too.

Well I still had some hope because there was a third baby cactus on the other side of the big one. Every day when I cleaned my teeth I peeped at it to see if it had got a face. At last it got one and opened its mouth and said I could have a wish. I saw now I could have had three wishes if I hadn't spoiled the first two. I had to be very careful. I said,

"I wish that more baby cactuses will grow, one every week."

"And will you always water my mum only not too much?"

Of course I said yes, and the baby cactus grickled (that's a prickly grin) and said okay, you got it. After that a new cactus bud grew every week on the big one and gave me a wish and soon we had a big flat with a view and <u>alot</u> of other things that I wished for my mum, and I wished a beautiful real silver bowl for the mother cactus to grow in. And now it's up to the sealing and the baby buds have turned into flowers and we're rich and don't have to save any more. (392 words.)

There now, you see you could write a nice story with nothing sinister about it. A+. _Except, if I ever see you write "a lot" as one word again, it will definitely be a D!_ You wouldn't write "alittle" or "afew" or "abit," would you? Now copy it out again in your _best writing_ (print) and I'll send it off for you to the competition. Good luck!

Special ~~SCHOOL~~ PRIVATE NOTEBOOK

I haven't written in here for a long time. I had my birthday. I only wanted one thing – a new pet. I read somewhere that if you want a little pet you should start by asking for a horse. I asked for a dog which I knew would be a no and then I asked for a cat, no again, Mum said she's alerjic to cats, and then for a white rat. Mum shudered and said fine but then I'm leaving. I said a mouse then, how much smaller can a pet get? But Mum said now she's working any pet would be too much trouble and then it would die and she couldn't stand any more tears. She said, "Remember how you cried when your stupid Tamagochi pet died? It wasn't even alive!" I said I bet Gene would let me have a pet. I only menshon Gene when I'm really annoyed with Mum.

I only calmed down when Mum asked what I wanted for a birthday treat. Last year Gene helped us to give a wonderful party but I didn't want one in our little flat. I had to think what I wanted instead.

I thought Gene wouldn't send me anything but she did. She sent me a lovely card (she sent it to Mum's work adress, she doesn't know where we live now) and a dress from Monsoon. It was beautiful, dark red velvit with same colour satin stripes, but now I don't go to ballets and posh places any more I don't know when I'll wear it. Nobody wears dresses to parties. Last year I went to Nicola's birthday and we all had to dress up as one of the Power Babes. You could choose to be Girl Power, Man Power, High Power, Super Power or Nuclear Power. I went as High Power and I wore letherlook jeans that I bought from a charity shop and I borrowed Peony's pogostick to be high (of course I didn't stay on it the whole party). There was a disco and we danced to "I wanna be a sexy single". Nicola's dad told her mum we all waggled our bottoms like a bunch of little tarts. (Nicola heard and told us.)

For my birthday Gene gave me something else, a tape called Spoonface Steinberg. I loved that name and I could see from the picture it was about a girl my age. But she forgot we don't have a tape-machine. I used to listen to all the tapes she gave me on car rides.

Anyway for my treat I asked Mum to take me to a

play at the Polka Children's Theatre in Wimbledon. She didn't want to. She hates doing things with me that Gene used to. I think she thinks it's giving in. But I said that was what I wanted for my birthday treat so in the end we took Nicola and Alexandra to see "The Odyssey". It was fantastic because I knew the whole story and could tell Mum what was coming. Gene would never let me do that, she used to cover her ears if I did it. Mum let me, but then I saw she was asleep. Her pills have worked and her illness is alot (A LOT) better but she gets so tired she often falls asleep after work and at weekends and it's very annoying sometimes when I want to do things with her and the Odyssey was so good I didn't want her to miss any. Alexandra and Nicola thought the play was brilliant. They'd never seen a play in a real theatre before. I couldn't believe it. I've seen loads. Plays are different to anything else because it's really happening and things can go wrong so it's more exciting.

Nan sent Mum some money to buy me a present from her. She actually said she wanted me to have PIERCED EARS with gold rings!!! She knew I wanted that because I'd told her. But Mum said no <u>again</u>. She said pierced ears were dangerous that you could get an infexion or maybe even aids and anyway pierced ears are common. I was so frusterated I said "if common means ordinary, that's what we are," and she said "Common means working class, and that's what I'm _not_, not any more." I said "they're my ears" and she said "Not till you're SIXTEEN, till then they're mine." When I made a huge fuss Mum just went all quiet.

In the end she bought me something brilliant from her and Nan together, a tape deck for beside my bed. Now I can listen to my tapes. They're not all music, some of them are plays and stories Gene gave me. I love lots of them but my favourite is Spoonface Steinberg, the one Gene sent. It's about a little girl who's autistic and on top of that she's got canser. It's her thoughts. She's so clever, I think of her like Lisa Simpson only a real girl. Mum can't stand it. She got mad at Gene all over again for giving it to me. She said there's enough in real life to cry about, and it's true it's the saddest thing I've ever heard but I just love it. I've listened to it about a hundred times.

* * *

Yesterday when I came out of school Peony was waiting. She was wearing a big blue t-shirt with the whole front cut out of it except just the bit round the neck, so it hung like a cloak, and another one underneath with a monster face on it, like peeping out. She'd put lipstick on him. She had big white gloves like Krusty the Clown. AND she had a bike. She said to come to the shops with her. I said I wasn't allowed and she said "Mama's little babykin, rapped up in a rabbit skin." I just walked away but she came after me and followed me home.

Usually Peony's fun to play with even if she's a tease, but she just wanted me to help her learn to ride the bike and I wouldn't so then she sulked. I said we had to be indoors. She came but she wouldn't talk. I took her into the bedroom and then she started messing about with Mum's things. I got nervous and tried to get her into the living room to watch telly but she wouldn't come so I had to stay in the bedroom with her and she said "don't you trust me?" and started teasing, pretending to hide things up her sweater.

Then she gave me this funny look she has, out of the side of her eyes, and said "I couldn't hide <u>the bike</u>

144

there." I asked what she ment and she said "I nicked it from outside the bike shop." I said "you did not" and she said "Please don't call me a lier." Then I sort of believed her and felt scared in case the police had followed her.

I wished she'd go home but she didn't so I just ignored her and put one of Gene's tapes on. It was a funny story about two twin girls, called Angela and Diabola, one of them good and one really really bad, and Peony got interested. After she'd listened a bit she started laughing and said, "I suppose you think you're the good one and I'm the bad one." I said "well maybe you are the bad one because Diabola has no conscience and you haven't either or you couldn't steal a bike."

Peony didn't say anything and then she said "I was having you on, Mum gave me the bike." I said, "I bet you'd steal my mum's things if I wasn't here." And then she got really insulted and said "I'm not a thief, I only nick from shops." I said "It's still stealing and it makes the shops charge more to make up for it (which is what Gene told me)." She said "how did you get to be such a goody-goody?" and <u>just then</u> the bad twin on the tape got mad and said to her sister "You icky sticky creepy crawlie little <u>goody-goody</u>"

145

which is my favourite bit on the whole tape, and Peony hung her mouth open and then we just fell on the floor laughing.

Then I felt more friendly with her and read her my cactus story. She said it was <u>dead soppy</u>. She said magic was rubbish. I told her about the competition and she said "I bet if you wrote a proper story with no magic in, you'd win. Write one about me." I said what about and she said, "pretend I really stole the bike and got caught and then read it to me and I'll make you take out the soppy bits."

She left before Mum came home. I didn't want to tell Mum she'd been but Mum noticed all her things had moved so I had to. She <u>well</u> told me off for letting Peony in and she said I wasn't to invite <u>anyone</u> home when she's not here. She was furious about Peony messing with her things and said I mustn't play with her, she said even Sharon said Peony was a bit wild.

Her own mum said that, and she doesn't even know about Peony going on the rob. And Mum doesn't know that we went outside and I helped hold Peony on her bike either. When it was <u>getting dark</u>. She'd go spare if she knew that. But nothing happened to us and it was fun.

The Girl Who Robbed a Bike

by Alice Williamson-Stone

Poppy was a thief which she had to be because she didn't have a family. Her dad died and she had three little brothers to look after and she was only nine. She knew Social Services would take the boys away if she let them. So they lived in a shed in a garden and no one knew they were there. (No one lived in the house it was in.)

She went on the rob everyday for food. She robbed baked beans and bread and pot noodles and apples and sweets and milk for the baby. She made picnics for them in the shed and in the garden which was over grown and had high fences. She made them all be very quiet. They played no-noise games like grandmother's steps and hide-and-seek (silent counting and no I'm coming). At night she tucked them up in sleeping bags and told them stories in a wisper. They did everything wispering even when they cried for their dad. When the baby cried they all lay on top of him and said "SHHHHH!"

Poppy dreamed of a bicicle with a basket so she could do the robbing easier and go whizing along if someone chased her which they often did. She went to a bicicle shop and told the man she wanted to try out one of the bikes. The man said,

"How do I know you'll bring it back?"

She said,

"You can come with me on your bike." So they went for a ride and suddenly Poppy whized through a red light and nearly got killed by the cars crossing the crossing but she just about didn't, and the bike man couldn't chase her and she got away and came home.

One of her brothers thought she was brilliant and she taught him to ride in the back ally behind the shed. Her other brother said "What would Dad say if he knew you'd nicked it" and that made her conscience hurt and she was cross and forgot to wisper, "You don't mind when I rob food for you" and he said

"But a bike's different, that's a wanna have not a gotta have. Dad said you have to know the difference and that stealing's wrong."

Poppy wouldn't speak to him but that night she dreamt her dad saying "Take the bike back Poppy." So very early in the morning she started to ride the bike back to the shop (before it opened) but when she got there a policeman was waiting. He grabbed her and said "I'm feeling your coller!" (He ment he arrested her.) She tried to run but he put handcuffs on that were very heavy and took her to the police station and put her in a cell with bars and she was so scared. He said, "Where do you live and what are your parents called?" But of course she couldn't answer.

She sat in the cell and fell into dispair because she knew she would be there for ever because who would come to get her out? But someone did come, it was the bicicle shop man. He said "You should be ashamed to be a thief, I hope they put you away for a long long time" and she said "It's not fair because I was only looking after my brothers." And he said

"What brothers, tell me all about it."

So she did and he told them to let her out of the cell and she took him to the shed and he looked at the boys and said "I have always wanted a family." The boys' names were Tommy, Clifford and James by the way, James was the baby. He took them home with him and said they could call him Dad and after that Poppy didn't have to go on the rob any more.

I looked up all the words I wasn't sure of and I don't think I made a single spelling mistake. I read it out loud to myself and copied it two times in my ultimate best cursive to make it perfect and then I asked Brandy if I could have a form for the competition. She said "But I've sent your story in" and I said "I've written another story." She said can I see it and I said I'd rather just send it. So she gave me a form and I read the rubric and filled it in, with my name kept seprate from the story. Then I read it to Peony.

I really thought she'd go for it. But when I'd finished she said, "It's max till the end. The end stinks." I said why, and she said "Because it's soppy. You're so soppy Alice, you think everything comes out all hotsy-totsy all the time but it doesn't. It should have a sad ending like Spoonface to be more real." (This gives away that I'd let her in the flat again and played more tapes with her which makes another secret.) When she said Spoonface I thought she might be right because Spoonface dies. I said "How would you end it?" and she said, "The bicicle man should adopt the three boys because he's a man but he wouldn't want Poppy." I was <u>well</u> offended and I said, "How do you know what he'd do," and she said, "Like my dad took my little brother with him when he left but he didn't want me."

So I changed it and made Poppy end up as a begger child in the streets with a card saying

> HOMELESS AND
> HUNGRY

without even her little brothers. She cried terribly but no one even gave her any money. In the end I sort of pulled back like a movie camera in the writing, and left her sitting there all alone.

Then I had to go to the post office for a postal order for the £2 to enter the competition and 50p for two big envelopes and 68p for stamps. So I couldn't go straight home from school, I had to go to the shops which are the other way. And even then I didn't come straight back. I walked around a bit all by myself and tried to imagine I was Poppy with no home and having to beg money. Once I sat down on the ground outside a shop <u>just for a minute</u> to see how it felt but when people looked at me I jumped up again, it felt so awful and deplorable.

Then I rushed home and read my story out loud one last time with the new ending, and I started crying it was so sad. It's funny I don't mind crying over Spoonface but she was someone else's. Poppy was mine. I thought of the gods like Zeus. I had power, I could change it, I could make things come out right for Poppy. I wondered how the person who wrote Spoonface could have let her die, they must have been very hard hearted. I couldn't leave Poppy like that so I went back to my old ending. Of course I had to copy it all out <u>again</u>. I was <u>well</u> fed up with Peony specially as I thought she maybe was right about my ending, it was a bit soppy but I <u>couldn't</u> leave Poppy a begger girl.

Then I had to go out again to post it and it was such a lovely day I got my bike out and went for a ride round the block all by myself. Nothing bad happened except I wobbled and made an old lady go off the pavement but I said sorry and she said, "Don't worry love, we all had to learn. You should get a bell to worn people."

Special PRIVATE
~~SCHOOL~~ NOTEBOOK

This is the first time I've written in my ortobiography for nearly three months. And that's because I nearly died, and that's not made up. While I'm writing this I'm thinking, I nearly didn't write these words. I nearly wasn't in the world any more. If you don't believe in heaven that is a very scary thought. Maybe even if you do.

Mum told me I ought to write about what happened to me. She said write it just for yourself if you don't want anyone else to read it. I'm going to write it in here and then I may show it to Mum, I don't know yet. I know who I will show it to and that's Peony because without her I wouldn't be here.

Background. Peony started meeting me nearly every day after school and we'd do things. I never went on the rob with her but we did go to the shops. She learnt to ride her bike and then she wanted us to go to the park. It was a long way but she said we'd be

OK and she kept on at me until I did. Luckily Gene had given me a Swatch watch so I always knew when to go home so Mum wouldn't know. Of course we rode on the pavement but when we had to cross a side road she rode and I walked and pushed my bike and she always laughed and made rabbit's ears at me. So in the end I rode across too.

We took picnics in my basket. I bought things like sosage rolls with my pocket money and Peony robbed some choclate bars. At first I wouldn't eat them but one day we were sitting on the grass and she pushed me over and pushed a Dime bar into my mouth and made me taste it. After that I ate them sometimes. I never knew how I felt about Peony. I liked her but I was sort of scared of her because she was wild, but she was never boring.

We fratched alot (A LOT), she said I was snobby and a goody-goody, and sometimes we didn't speak and she didn't come after school for a bit. But then she'd turn up again. I never told Mum about her because I knew Mum would say she was a bad influance. So that was another secret.

Peony talked a lot about her school. It's a regular state school, not like my private one, and she said it was pretty grotty. But she likes her teacher who's a man. Brandy's strict and makes us work and sometimes I can't stand her but Peony likes her teacher because he makes them laugh. He's always telling jokes, like "Why are there no asparin in the jungle? Because paracetemol." (Parrots eat em all – she had to explain it.) Still maybe it's better to have a strict teacher. I found out why Peony likes me to read to her, is because she doesn't read very well herself.

Once Peony and me talked about not having dads, she said she hated her dad for leaving her mum and her, and I said I didn't hate my dad because I'd never seen him. Then I told her about the photo I stole and I showed it to her. I thought she'd say something sneery but she didn't. She said he looked really nice. Next day she brought me one of her and her little brother and her dad and her mum all together. They were all laughing and he had his arms round them. I never thought till I saw that how there was not one photo of Mum and Dad and me as a family.

Peony's dad and mum were married and he lived with them before he left them so that makes a difference. Still when I thought about it I thought maybe I <u>should</u> hate Dad for not loving Mum even if you can't order love (as Mum says). I still don't understand why they did sex together if he didn't love her but in films lots of people do. Maybe he thought he did.

Anyway Peony saved my life. Cos one day in May we were out in the park and I'd been feeling funny all day and once I'd gone to the toilet to throw up at school and I didn't want to go to the park but Peony wanted to cos it was such a nice day.  May's my best month. All the greens are still different (I did a picture of trees in May in Art and I used five different green crayons, two yellow and a sort of red).

It was so hot we took off our tops. We were lying on the grass and Peony said "Look at the chestnut candles, all pink and white, you'd like drawing them" and I tried to look up but I couldn't because the sun hurt my eyes. I felt all sick and spinny and I just lay there by my bike and wouldn't eat our picnic or play and Peony said "What's wrong with you, you look really bad," and then she said "what's that on your chest? It looks like a beetle." I tried to look down but

I couldn't move my neck and I suddenly felt really, really scared. I put my hands over my eyes and started to cry and I felt Peony touching my chest.

Then I don't remember anything for a bit and then I felt something wet on my face. I tried to open my eyes and saw a little dog licking me and then I saw a woman beside me doing something to my chest and there were voices calling and someone picked me up and next thing I knew I was in the ambulance. I knew it was one because I could hear the siron but I was really out of it. I don't remember much after that except it hurt a lot and whenever I woke up (sort of) it was horrible and muddly and I was all joined up to tubes and stuff. But I wasn't really awake much for a long long time.

What had happened was, Peony saw some big blackish spots and she'd seen this programme on TV and her teacher had talked about it at school so she called to a woman who was passing and said "I think my friend's got meningitis" and the woman did the glass test with her glasses (you press glass against the spots and if they don't go white you've got it) and then she called the ambulance with her mobile phone and that saved my life.

I was in the hospital in intensive care for six

weeks. And after that I wasn't so out of it because I was getting better. I got hundreds of get well cards, I couldn't believe how many, nearly everyone at my school sent one or a class one. And I missed prize giving. Not that I was going to win anything but I wanted to see Gene. I wanted to see her so much. Sometimes when I was ill I thought I really saw Gene but I was so out of it I knew at the time it wasn't real.

When I was very ill before I started to get better I dreamed about prize giving. My dream was she stood on the school stage and I waved to her and said to everyone "That's my grandma." But she didn't reconise me or pretended not to and I felt all crazy and ran up on to the stage shouting "Give me a prize, give me a prize!" even though I hadn't won one. I dreamed that dream about a hundred times. So I was releeved as well as disappointed not to be at prize giving in case that really happened.

But one day when I was getting really better, Miss Brand came to see me and said there was good news. I'd won third prize in the competition, with my Poppy story, not the cactus one. £30!!!! Brandy said the brilliant thing was I won in the 10 to 14's when I was only just ten and my story would be published in a special booklet with all the winners in. Then she said, "So you'll be a published auther Alice, and I have to confess that your cursive handwriting was specially comended."

Then something really really strange happened. Into my head came these words "Gene would be proud of me." And at the <u>same time</u>, just like when Peony and me heard the tape of Angela and Diabola, Mum said, "Gene is very proud of you." I was surprised and said "How does she know?" and Mum said, "Because I told her." And I said, "Does she know I've had meningitis?" and Mum said "Of course, she came to see you a lot and sat by your bed, don't you remember that at all?" I shook my head and Brandy said, "She was great at prize giving, Alice, and she menshoned you in her speech. She said she was your grandma and that you were one of her favourite people in the world and asked us all to pray for you to get well."

I just boggled my eyes at her. I knew that couldn't be true. I said, "She didn't say pray." Brandy thought about it and said, "Well, perhaps she said "send lots of cards and think strong get-well thoughts." And then I believed it because Gene wouldn't say pray but she would say about strong thoughts, she believes in those.

Then I knew why I'd got so many cards. And that I'd really seen Gene and that my horrible dream was rubbish. Gene would never not reconise me. I was thinking about that so much. Then Brandy gave me a kiss and said, "I'm going to miss your weird stories." She ment because we won't have her next year.

Peony said if I'd done the begger girl Spoonface type ending to my Poppy story I'd have won first prize instead of only third. She says things never come out all hotsy-totsy. I don't want to believe that. Maybe it's true sometimes but it's not true always. It can't be.

When I came out of hospital I knew things were going to change. For one thing I've sort of had to learn to walk again because the meningitis did something to my toes. I know I'm lucky it wasn't my fingers or that I didn't die but I hate them. I even put my face flannel over them in the bath. I don't think I'll ever go swimming again, people would stair and make remarks. (I can still ride my bike though.)

But still I thought I'd have two grandmothers again and that things with Gene would be the same as they'd been before the Big Row, but it didn't exactly happen.

Mum was so desprit when I was ill she thought nothing else mattered. She rang Gene up and told her about my meningitis and Gene came from the country to be with me. Grandad came. Nan came from Liverpool. But this is what I can't stop thinking about. Even my dad came. He and Johanna came all the way from Holland when they thought I was going to die. But when I didn't he went back again.

I couldn't believe it when Mum told me that. I couldn't believe it that he'd come and I couldn't believe it that he'd gone again without me seeing him. I was inconsoulable. I yelled at Mum, "Why didn't you keep him here? Why didn't you wake me up? Why didn't you make him love you?" Mum said, "I'm sorry, Alice. I would have tied him up to keep him here for you but his life is in Holland and besides, Johanna is going to have a baby." (Yes, she said that then, and I didn't even notice I was in such a state!)

I said, "did Gene tell him to go back?" and she said "I don't know. But I wouldn't blame her. If he tried to be your dad properly it would be like trying to be two people in two places. He would mess up his life and maybe yours too." I shouted "It wouldn't mess up my life, that's crazy," and she said, "Well crazy or not that's the way it is and we both have to accept it."

I shouted at her more. I knew it was unfair to

blame her but I couldn't stand it that he'd been next to my bed and held my hand and I never knew it and now he was back in Amsterdam. I was sure then that Peony's right and happy endings don't happen.

And then Mum told me a few things about money. While Gene was friends with us she put money in some trust thing for my school fees but she's stopped adding to it now. There's enough in it for three or four years at my school and after that Mum'll have to start paying and it's <u>thousands of pounds a year</u>. AND I found out that Mum's still paying back money she borrowed from the bank for studying to be a solicitor. So maybe we'll never have any money and have to go on living in this poky little flat for ever.

One good thing happened, all the secrets came out. First Mum found out about me meeting Peony and not going straight home, because I was in the park when my meningitis happened, and then I told her the other secrets that I'd done. It's quite good nearly dying in a way because nobody bothers about little things. (So long as you don't actully, of course.)

Special ~~SCHOOL~~ PRIVATE NOTEBOOK

I think last night I saw Gene for the last time for a long time anyway. I'm miserable so I'll write it out of myself. It's night and I'm writing in bed with my torch because I'm ment to be asleep but I can't.

She asked Mum if she could take me out just once more. Mum brought me to a meeting place outside Lester Square tube station. She and Gene were polite but not friendly. I thought of The Parent Trap and I wanted to grab them and drag them together but I remembered what Mum said about limitations so what was the point.

Gene said we could go to a Pizza Hut if I liked which was nice of her because she hates pizzas, and once I would've but I thought it was a special occasion so we went to a posh place she likes called the Ivy which is for actors and I had rice with tomato sorce (but it was special) and she said woops, here goes more mad cow disease, and had a big steak and there were candles and flowers and the waiter knew her and was very smily to us and gave me a whole box of delishus sweets called petty fours to take home.

We talked and talked. She told me about Copper's puppies that are grown-up now, but she kept one and called him Al. I thought it was after me but she said no, it was after a gangster called Al  Capone because he is such a roughian. Then she confessed that when Mum told her I might die, she'd speeded again in her car only the police didn't catch her this time, and I told her about Peony and my story and the hospital, and then I told her about my feet, but she knew most of it already.

I asked her something I hadn't asked Mum because of her and men, which was if she thought a boy could fancy me with my feet being ugly. Gene said, "Show them to me at once, I want to see them now." So I took off my shoes under the table and put my feet in Gene's lap under her napkin and then I suddenly paniced and snatched them away or I tried to, and said "Don't look don't look" but she grabbed my ankels and said "Shut up." She looked down at them and stroked them and said "They aren't ugly at all, they're just a little bit different and any boy who wouldn't fancy you because of that isn't worth a row of beans." Then she looked straight in my eyes and said, "I <u>promise</u> you, you'll meet someone who you'll be very scared of telling for fear he won't fancy you, and then you will tell and he'll say, Alice, you do menshon the most irevelent things." (I think it was that, anyway it means things that don't matter.)

She said she has something wrong with her, too (only she didn't tell me what) and that Grandad said that, when she first told him. She said a boy who loves you won't give a dam about your poor darling feet, except maybe he'll love you all the more. And I put my shoes back on and we had some delishus sweet things called profiteroles. And then she took me to see a cartoon movie about Moses because we'd started to learn about Ancient Egypt when I left school.

She used to say Mum takes me to too scary films but this one was scarier than Batman! All those poor slaves getting whiped and Moses turning the Nile to blood (how did the people drink?) and the other plages, and when God killed all the first born Egyptians I hated it because I'm a first born and I thought God should have had a bad conscience, much worse than Theseus, all <u>he</u> did was leave Ariadne on the island and he wasn't even a god.

When I said that to Gene when we came out she laughed a lot and hugged and kissed me and said I was a wonderful child and that my Mum was doing a pretty good job. I said "So why don't you like her?" and she said, "Darling, I am what I am and she is what she is. You don't know everything. I can't keep my mouth shut where you're concerned and I think you and your mum are better off without me." I said, "But why can't you just be a grandma?" and she didn't say anything while we walked down the street with all the bright lights and traffic going by and I thought she'd forgotten but then she said a weird thing. She said, "Do you know what, Alice? I think I've been trying to be your father all this time."

I laughed so loud people turned to stair at me but then I stopped because I thought of all the times she did sporty things with me like run after me on my bike (and when I could ride she rode with me on Grandad's bike and once she fell off into the nettly hedge and I had to ride to fetch Grandad to pull her up and she was stung all over) and lead me on Biddy, all up the hills for an adventure, and teach me to swim and go on scary rides (Thunder Mountain) and stuff and teasing me when I wasn't brave. Sometimes I've been upset with Gene because she teased me and made me do things I was scared to do but now I'm glad. I'd never've done them without her.

I remembered when I was listening to Gene and Grandad talking about my dad and I thought maybe Gene was sorry for me not having a dad to teach me to be brave and do sporty things. She <u>was</u> sort of like a dad in a way.

That's why I stopped laughing. Because of course she could never be my dad but it was sort of nice of her to try.

Then she said, "Mum won't give me your adress. But I know her work adress and I'll write to you there and we can keep in touch if you like." And I thought she still loves me to distraxion and maybe she'd like to come back to us but if Mum won't even tell her our new adress it's Mum who wants her not to.

When we met Mum they didn't say much, but Gene hugged and kissed me again and we were both crying. I turned round as we walked towards the tube and waved and Gene stood there with her yellow hair in the lighted-up night street in the crowd. She didn't wave back, she just stood still and looked after us till we turned the corner.

Mum was all withdrawn going home (or maybe it was me) but when we got here she said "Well, how was it?" I said good, but I felt a lot sad and a bit angry. She said "Are you angry with me? I suppose you think I lost you your grandma." Which I did think and I said, "It's you who doesn't want Gene now, isn't it," and she said "I don't want her or her money. You can use the trust later, if you want to, but I can't afford a private education for you. I've found an ordinary school for you, a local one, the one Peony goes to."

I got a real shock. I thought of Brandy saying she'd miss my weird stories. And I thought of Peony telling me about her grotty school. I blew up right away and said "I don't want to leave my school!" and Mum said, "You've left it, Alice." I said how could you, without telling me, and she said "I didn't want to upset you till you were completely better. Listen Alice, we have to stand on our own feet. Gene kept saying I made all the choices. Well, I chose to have you and I'm glad I did, but then this is how it has to be. Just you and me. I thought it could be different but I was wrong. But we'll manage. I promise."

I wasn't nice. I wish I had been, now, because I know she had a really rough time when I was ill. But I carried on about how I wouldn't have had to go to a grotty school if we still had Gene, so Mum made me go to bed because I was giving her a guilt trip. So I went and cried in bed and then I started writing and only stopped when I heard the TV go off. But by morning I'd calmed down. Because when I thought about what she'd said about choosing me and about standing on our own feet I felt kind of proud in a way, like we were two heroins.

But then I started thinking properly about Johanna and Dad having a baby. It makes everything worse. It's bad enough not seeing Dad but now that means not seeing my little brother or sister (half) the only one I'll ever have because <u>for sure</u> Mum's never going to have one.

It's just not fair. Mum often says life isn't fair but it <u>ought</u> to be and if there was really a God, or even gods like the Greeks had, it would be, or at least you could complain. I've always wanted a brother or sister. I'll just have to make do with seeing my cousin James once in a long while, and dream about the other one. Only James is boring.

* * *

I wanted to phone Gene like I used to but I couldn't so I held back till I got to Sharon's. Sharon child-minds me all day during the holidays, only she doesn't do much minding, she knits on her knitting machine or even goes out, and lets us do what we like. I <u>should</u> tell Mum what a bad minder she is but then I wouldn't have Peony to play with.

I told her about going to her school and she said "Do you good, you won't be so snobby then." I said "Will you go on being my friend even if I'm older?" and she said yes if I'd write more stories about her, really scary spooky ones with sad vilent endings. I said like what, and she said, "like I get put in a dunjon and bricked up and die of hunger and become a skeleton." I thought that would make a brilliant story so I said OK I will then, and I could make you come back as a scary goste and hornt the people who put you in the dunjon. She got excited and said YES and they'd go mad and jump off bridges and I said out of sky-scrapers and she said out of airoplanes and I said off the moon and she said off Venus and we just got histerical laughing and I felt A LOT better. It's really great to have a friend like Peony who's never boring not to menshon saves your life.

Even with Peony though it can get boring being at

Sharon's all day, and sometimes we sneak out and play in the street or even go to the shops. I think I've stopped Peony robbing or at least she doesn't do it in front of me. Or we watch TV, or she does while I write, like now. I'm trying not to think of Gene and being in the country and swimming and riding and playing with Copper. And Al. I almost want it to be the end of holidays and time to go to my new (grotty) school.

Later. I've just drawn a cactus like in my cactus story. It has the wishes on it that I'd make if my story was true. One of the cactus buds is the new baby all curled up still and not born. One is my dad. One is Gene and there's a cross-looking one for Grandad and one is Copper. One is a house with a garden. Then I drew a pair of feet. I made them like mine but then I made them perfect. It's a wish-cactus after all.

I love magic and when I draw I believe in it. But I know Peony's right really, you have to manage without it. The only real-life magic is writing and drawing. It's like, when you write about bad things and worries or draw them they get paler or go right out of your body and on to the paper.

I can even make myself laugh. I drew a last cactus bud. It's Peony as a scary skeleton, it looks really funny. She loves it and wants me to do a big one for her room. I'll do one dressed up in one of her crazy hats!

But first I'm going to start writing the story about the dunjon. I wonder what my new teacher will think of my cursive.

THE DUNJON AND THE GOSTE

by Alice Williamson-Stone

In the olden days there was a castle in Scotland called Castle Deeps. It was called that because the man who built it, before he built it dug a great deep hole in the top of a hill and built the castle on top of that. His name was Ronald McDonald and he was a bad cruel man.

One day when his great castle was finished he got bored and went to China to fight a war. He won the war and brought back with him lots of nice silk things like shirts and curtains and as well he brought back a little slave-girl he'd captured. Her name was Peony which is a Chinese flower.

Peony had to live in the cold castle and do jobs for Ronald McDonald. Like she had to polish his riding boots and bring him tea on a dainty tray (China tea of course which he'd brought back and she knew how to make) and run errands to the shops and keep his suits of armour oiled. She worked all the time and at night she had to sleep in a tiny room in the top of the castle which was very cold and dreary. She didn't speak any Scottish and had no one to talk to and just did what she was told all the time and was dredfully homesick for China and her family. Ronald McDonald never let her have Chinese take-away, he made her eat bear meat and other Scottish food like porridge with lumps in.

One night she couldn't stand it because Ronald McDonald had been shouting at her because the tea wasn't strong enough and she'd left a smudj on his boots. So she cut off her long black pigtail and twisted the hairs into a long rope and climed down it to escape.

But there below was the mote which was like a river going right around the castle, and Ronald McDonald was swimming in it. He saw Peony climing down and he swam to her and grabbed her.

"How dare you run away from my castle!" he shouted. "Now you will go to my dunjon and you will never come out alive!"

Poor little Peony was taken down a lot of stairs into the big deep hole under the castle which was the dunjon. It was full of spiders and beetles and stijian gloom. She heard wicked Ronald McDonald locking the iron door with a big key. Then he shouted, "Now I will throw this key into the mote!" And Peony knew she would never come out of the dunjon but would die down there alone in the dark.

And she did. But first she scratched a vow on the wall in Chinese letters.

One night Ronald McDonald heard rattling noises coming from the dunjon. He knew Peony must've died long ago so he opened the door (he hadn't really thrown the key away, he just said that to make Peony dispair) and then he got a big fright. Inside the door was a little skeleton standing rattling at him and wagging its jaw. He screamed and fainted.

That was just the beginning. When he came to, the little skeleton was gone, but that night he heard chains clanking and keys turning and strange cries and grones. But most of all he heard the rattling of bones. He couldn't sleep. He was afraid to get out of bed. In the days he tried to forget it but he couldn't. All he could think about was Peony left alone in the dunjon and at last after many terrible nights he made himself go down there.

"I'll bury her skeleton" he said to himself. "That'll be the end of it."

But when he went down there was no skeleton, but he saw some Chinese writing on the wall. It was Peony's vow. He knew some Chinese from when he'd been there, and now he read it. He was full of dred.

"I will come back and hornt my cruel master to his last hour."

He fell back in a faint. While he was fainted, there was a creak and the door slowly closed. When he came to it was quite dark. He got to the door and tried to open it. Then he fell to the floor with a grone.

He'd left the key on the outside.

(And that's no soppy ending, I don't care what anybody says.)

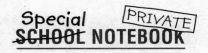

Special ~~SCHOOL~~ NOTEBOOK PRIVATE

October

Wait till I see Peony at school tomorrow! Something fantastic and incredable has happened!

Here is the letter Mum gave me when she got home from work tonight. It was adressed to me at Gene's house, and Gene sent it on to Mum's work adress. I'm going to stick it in here! I'm so excited I've forgotten where I put the glue so I'll use selotape.

Dear Alice,

This is Johanna writing to you, I suppose I am a sort of step-mother for you but I am not a wicked one.

I have so much wanted to write to you before this. You know your dad and I are going to have a baby and we think for a long time we may want that it will be born in England. Now we have decide definitely. The child is due on Christmas Day so we are coming next month (November) to make ready for it.

That was one reason why we needed to have our house back. I felt bad Gene ask you to leave but we haven't got a lot of money and where else could we live?

When your dad saw you in the hospital he had suddenly some very strong feelings about you. We both want to get to know you. And if you would agree, we want to share the baby with you.

Your dad has tried to write to you but he doesn't know what to say. He feels shy because although you are his daughter, he doesn't know you. But he will get over it. Men are better at talking face to face than for writing letters. He wants very much to get to know you, though it won't happen all at once.

Please share this letter with your mother. I'll write again when we get to London and I hope by then you will get used to the idea of to have a bigger family.

I can't sign myself "Love, Johanna" yet because we don't know each other. But I am rather sure I am going to love you, so I will sign
Love that comes in future,
Johanna

I nearly went crazy when I read this letter. I loved all the mistakes! I kissed the page and pretended it was both of them and then I ran around the flat shouting and laughing and every time I passed Mum I hugged her and twerled her around. After a while I calmed down and then Mum said, "Yes, I'm glad, it's very good news for you, Alice." I said it's better than good. Mum didn't say anything.

I said "isn't it good news for you too?" and she said, "Well it could be." She had that funny look and I had a heartsink because I remembered about her wanting to get Dad and not being able to because he lived in

Holland. I said, "You won't give his name to the DSS will you?" Mum said, "I might. Don't you want a nicer place to live?" I said, "But you said we'd stand on our own feet! He needs his money for Johanna and the baby." Mum looked at me a long time. "Whose side are you on?" she said. I said, "You can have all my trust money, but don't snitch on Dad, it'll make trouble and I want things to be nice."

Mum said, "I'm not making any promises. Nobody told him to go and make another family when he's never given us a penny."

I came in here then to write this. To help me think. <u>Why</u> is everything so complicated? Why does <u>everything</u> have a downside? I've just thought. Even telling Peony I'm getting my dad back might make her jelous. And if I told her about what Mum said, she'd sing her favourite TV ad, "there may be truuuuble ahead".

But I can't help it, I just feel so happy, I'm not going to let anything spoil it. And I'm going to be the best half-sister any baby ever had and I'm not going to let anything bad or complicated happen to himher, herhim. Babies aren't complicated, they're simple, it's just grown-ups that make things complicated for them.

AND if I see my dad, and see the baby, I bet I'll see Gene too, she won't be able to help seeing me because we'll both be her grandchildren. And she won't need to try to be my dad any more.

She will be our grandma. Just that.

THE
INDIAN
IN THE
CUPBOARD

Lynne Reid Banks

*Neither Omri nor the Indian moved for perhaps a minute and
a half. They hardly breathed either. They just stared at each
other.*

At first, Omri is unimpressed with the plastic Indian toy
he is given for his birthday. But when he puts it in his old
cupboard and turns the key, something extraordinary
happens that will change Omri's life for ever. For Little
Bull, the Iroquois Indian brave, comes to life...

The first book in the magical series about
Omri and Little Bull

An imprint of HarperCollins*Publishers*

RETURN
OF THE
INDIAN

Lynne Reid Banks

*…Lying face-down across the pony's back was a limp, motionless
form. It was Little Bull.*

Omri can't resist bringing the small people back to life
again. But when the cupboard door opens, Omri finds
Little Bull unconscious with two bullet wounds in his
back. As Omri tries to help him, he faces the terrifying
responsibility of power – the power of life and death…

The second book in the magical series about
Omri and Little Bull

An imprint of HarperCollinsPublishers

Lynne Reid Banks

Twins are meant to be alike but Angela and Diabola are
opposites in every way.
Angela is completely good;
Diabola is pure evil.

Everyone loves Angela;
even the vicar is terrified of Diabola.

As Diabola's powers grow, it seems that no one can
stop her. Only Angela seems to know what goes on
in her twin's mind…

An imprint of HarperCollinsPublishers

Order Form

To order direct from the publishers, just make a list of the titles you want and fill in the form below:

Name ....

Address ....

....

....

Send to: Dept 6, HarperCollins Publishers Ltd, Westerhill Road, Bishopbriggs, Glasgow G64 2QT.

Please enclose a cheque or postal order to the value of the cover price, plus:

UK & BFPO: Add £1.00 for the first book, and 25p per copy for each additional book ordered.

Overseas and Eire: Add £2.95 service charge. Books will be sent by surface mail but quotes for airmail despatch will be given on request.

A 24-hour telephone ordering service is available to holders of Visa, MasterCard, Amex or Switch cards on 0141- 772 2281.

An imprint of HarperCollins*Publishers*